A WICKED

SEA

BY EM BROWN

COPYRIGHT

A WICKED

SEA

PROLOGUE

*D*id she dare test his devotion? As Marinette La Croix stared across her captain's cabin into the icy-blue eyes of her first mate, as handsome as he was menacing, she wondered if she could trust any man. Even those brought up in gentle society proved only to be wolves in the gilded trappings of sheep.

She was no stranger to wolves, and her first mate made no attempts to hide the beast within. But Harry was a wounded beast, and those often proved the most dangerous.

He stared at her with obvious hunger. His ardor, as well as hers, always burned brightest after a pillage. At the moment, however, she was as much vexed as aroused. Harry needed to be punished. That he had now saved her life—twice—did not absolve him for disregarding a direct order.

A cautionary voice in her head told her not to push him too far, but she was disinclined to

5

regard it, as she was somehow wont to do when it came to Harry. But if she dared toy with the wolf, there was always the possibility that she would pay the price with her life.

CHAPTER ONE

~ 1715, High Seas of the West Indies ~

The man leaped from the shadows, catching La Croix off her guard. A hard object struck the side of her head, blurring her vision as she was forced to bite the wooden floor of the captain's quarters. Despite the blow to her body from her fall, she managed to grab the cutlass she had dropped.

But a heavy boot ground her wrist into the floor before she could lift her weapon. She let out a howl; if he applied any more pressure, the bones in her wrist would surely give.

The cutlass was ripped from her hand. She glanced up at her assailant, a burly sailor burnt orange from the sun. He was nearly thrice her size, but she relied upon her agility and swiftness to best the superior strength of his sex.

With her wrist still pinned beneath his boot, she pulled her right knee beneath her body and whipped her left leg around, striking his shin.

Surprised, he allowed his boot to come off her wrist. She rolled away from him as he attempted to bring the cutlass down upon her. She kicked at his arm, trying to dislodge her cutlass from his hold, but it seemed he was made of metal. Still holding the cutlass, he backhanded her with his other fist, knocking her off her feet once more. She fell against the captain's writing table, the many shells braided into her hair pelting the desk. Her tricorn fell over her eyes, and she tasted blood.

"Well, well," her assailant sneered, eying her from head to toe with disgust, "so much for the pirate bitch. Ye ain't so mighty and fearsome."

She tried to scramble back onto her feet, but he was before her, pressing the cutlass against her throat.

"My men have the ship," she informed him. "Surrender yourself now, and I might not tear the gizzards outta you alive before we keelhaul your ugly arse."

He stared at her, perhaps contemplating the truth of her words. Her men, the crew of the *Bloody Baron*, had mounted a successful attack upon the merchant vessel, whose crew and captain had been rounded and now awaited their fate on deck. Apparently, one of the crew members had hidden himself, attacking La Croix while she looked through the captain's silver.

She shut her eyes when the sailor chose to spit into her face for a response.

"Bloody cunt," he cursed. "I bet yer crew would trade the ship for their captain. Or would they be glad to be free from a bitch's command?"

Her men were busy loading the booty onto the *Bloody Baron* and guarding the merchant crew, but one of them was bound to come looking for her. If she could stall her assailant long enough, the ape wielding her cutlass would be outnumbered.

"*Mange la merde*," she returned.

He backhanded her across the face. Pain cracked the side of her head.

"I wonder what be worse: takin' orders from a wench or takin' orders from a nigre? Why, your crew might consider me their savior," the sailor continued with a grin that revealed stained and yellow teeth. "Doin' away with ye would give 'em back their cods, eh?"

She was not naive enough to think that none among her crew resented having her for a captain, but they all chose to serve her and the *Bloody Baron* of their own free will, for they fared as well under her command as they would under a Benjamin Hornigold or Stede Bonnet.

The ape's grin returned to a frown. "A female captain. What blarney. I wonder if you're even good for a fuck."

His gaze raked over her body. To disguise her form, she was heavily clothed in a shirt, waistcoat and coat. He grabbed her between her legs. If she did not fear for her life more, she would have burned at the violation.

"No cock or cods here," he said as he continued to grope her crotch. "I thought ye might have been trying to grow a pair."

She gritted her teeth as she contemplated what she could do. Perhaps she could offer her body as a distraction, but his touch made her want to retch.

He moved his paw up to her chest, searching for a breast. She kept her bosom bound to keep the mounds from swaying inconveniently. He squeezed what he could. Grabbing her by the front of her coat, he hauled her onto her feet and shoved her over the top of the writing table. She kicked at him, but he was quick for a large man, and once more had the cutlass at her throat.

"Let's see if your cunt be worth anything."

Deciding that she would rather die than be raped, she clawed at him, digging her nails into his hand, deep enough to draw blood.

With an oath, he retracted the cutlass long enough to deliver a right hook to the side of her face. Pain exploded in her cheek. She felt his hand at her breeches, ready to tear an opening in the crotch.

"Step away."

Though it hurt to breathe, she drew in a breath of relief. The cold, calm voice was that of Harry, her first mate.

Craning her neck, she saw him standing upon the threshold holding a pistol aimed at her assailant. Harry, a striking man but for his sunken, ghostly eyes that many found more unnerving than the metal hook that took the place of his right hand, had never looked finer to her.

The ape, startled at first, refused to be intimidated. He looked at the pistol. "Your shot might find its mark. But if not, your captain would be dead before you reloaded. Sure you wish to take that chance?"

For emphasis, he pushed the cutlass closer. The blade would have grazed her if she did not have a hold of his hand, pushing it away with all her might.

Harry cocked his head right, and his lips curled in amusement. She wanted to scream for Harry to shoot the man already. While many flintlocks could be unreliable, Harry had a rifled pistol with unparalleled accuracy, and she knew no better marksman. Her assailant was as good as dead.

"If my shot finds your heart," Harry said with agonizing slowness, "you'll die a swift death— more or less. If I miss, you'll bleed for hours before you die. Sure *you* wish to take that chance?"

Her assailant furrowed his brow, confused by the question.

A blast split the air, and she saw the sailor stumble back, dropping the cutlass, as blood stained his shoulder.

"Oh, dear. I missed," Harry drawled.

Scrambling off the table, La Croix grabbed her

cutlass and sliced the back of her assailant's leg. He cried out in pain as he stumbled to the floor. Harry approached the man and kicked him in the ribs. The sailor collapsed onto his back.

Harry turned to her. "Did he touch you?"

"He held me down. You saw that," she answered. Now that she was safe, she could feel aggravated at herself for needing to be rescued.

"No. Did he *touch* you?"

Wanting to move on and be done with the ship, she only stared at Harry. But he had his answer.

Turning back to the sailor, he drove his boot even harder into the man.

Though not unfamiliar with Harry's violent side, the fury with which he rained kicks upon the sailor surprised her.

To protect himself, the man turned onto his side and covered his head. Harry continued to kick him until, finding the backside an insufficient target, he bent down and hooked him by the shirtfront. Despite the man being much larger, Harry lifted him high enough to punch him in the face.

"Harry!" she barked, knowing her first mate

could take hours bludgeoning the sailor.

Dropping the sailor back onto the floor, Harry kicked at the man's head till blood coursed from the nose, mouth, and eyes.

"Desist!" she ordered.

As if he had not heard her, Harry continued to pummel the man, alternating between kicks and punches.

"Harry!" She yanked him back by the arm and gazed down at the sack of bloodied and blue flesh, curled in a fetal position. Harry's anger was suddenly contagious, and La Croix, realizing she had more cause to beat the sailor into oblivion, delivered her own kick to the man's bollocks. She pressed her boot down on his crotch just as he had upon her wrist. His hands, red and raw from protecting his head from Harry's assault, tried to keep her from crushing his cods.

Harry, meanwhile, had reloaded his pistol, which he aimed once more at the sailor. "D'you hope I find my mark this time?"

The sailor whimpered. He could only plead through his eyes.

Knowing that Harry probably intended to shoot the other shoulder, La Croix grabbed the pistol from him and fired the mercy of death into the sailor's chest.

"Here!" Harry protested. "I wasn't done with him."

She glared at him. "Yes, you are."

She did not understand the irritation that filled her, even as memories of a past rape taunted her mind. Turning around, she stalked out of the cabin, but not before hearing the crunch of bones as Harry brought his boot down upon the dead sailor's nose.

*****

Harry gently traced the split in her bottom lip with his thumb. "You're hurt."

La Croix swatted away his hand and spat blood into the basin atop the sideboard. They were back aboard the *Bloody Baron*, in the quiet of her cabin, but the vexation from earlier had not dissipated. Her head still throbbed, and to dull the pain, she grabbed the port taken from the captain's quarters of the merchant vessel.

Throwing herself into an armchair, she took a hearty gulp of the wine, wishing she could finish off the entire decanter, but, as a woman, she did not have the luxury of losing herself in blistering intoxication. She could never fully let down her guard. Even with Harry to protect her, she could not risk being in her cups. And while she trusted her first mate more than she trusted most anyone, he was a pirate. She would be a fool to trust one. And, pirate or no, no man could be fully trusted.

"I ought have hanged him by his cods for layin' a finger on ye," Harry said. His eyes, blue as the West Indies seas, were bright with intensity. They were always intense. They never even seemed to blink.

"Not worth the trouble," she dismissed, tossing her long dark hair, which she wore in dozens of plaited queues, over her shoulder. The plaits required little fussing, and the many shells woven into her hair made a distinctive—some deemed it ghastly—sound when she moved.

She propped her boots onto the footstool to appear more nonchalant than she felt. She rarely enjoyed reminders of the past, and the vision of her mother bent over a table beneath the bleeder who owned her at the time was her least favorite. Not even the report from her quartermaster of the bounty they had hauled could distract her from her discontent. Having taken over their target with the loss of only one man from her crew, a hundred pieces of eight to another crewmember for the loss of a finger, and minimal damage to her ship, she ought to have been celebrating.

"An example could have been made of him, a warning to others who would dare touch ye."

Although she was mildly amused that Harry was so protective of her, she knew he needed no reason to torture a fellow man. More often than not, she allowed Harry his fun, knowing that he could not vent his rage upon the man who had had his hand sliced off—Don Luis Chacón, Governor of Cuba.

And she wasn't sure if Harry was as much protective of her as he was possessive of her. As her first mate, he held an enviable position aboard her ship and was the only member of her crew she had ever allowed between her legs.

She surveyed him from head to foot to see that he had sustained no injury. The blood upon his gold-trimmed scarlet coat was not his own. She remembered when she had first laid eyes upon him in a tavern in Port Royal, thinking that he could not possibly be a pirate worth her spit, for he had all his teeth and looked far too pretty. At best he was a privateer in the pocket of the English.

He ought to have been dead.

She had had every intention of killing him. With his own precious pistol.

CHAPTER TWO

~ 1713, Port Royal ~

From her place of hiding behind a collection of shrubs beneath a palm tree, La Croix watched as the harlot, a bottle of rum in hand, approached Harry.

"That be quite the piece you have there," the wench said, taking a seat beside him on the beach, a balmy night breeze teasing her golden locks. Away from the docks, taverns and gambling houses, they relied upon the light of a moon near full and a few winking stars.

Harry spared her a glance, briefly resting with appreciation upon the swells above her décolletage, before returning to cleaning the barrel of his pistol. From the ease with which he used his hook, it was plain he'd had it for some time.

"But I warrant it not be as fine as your *other* piece." Her lashes lowered toward his crotch.

Harry snorted in amusement.

La Croix had her own pistol at her hip and could have shot him in the back then and there. But she wanted him to know why he was to meet death. The man had killed Olamide, her first mate and a brother, not by birth but by their shared African blood. Though she had been told the duel had been fair betwixt the men, that mattered little to her. She was convinced that Olamide had been tricked into settling a squabble in the manner of aristocratic gentlemen when fisticuffs would have done.

The wench leaned in closer, her shoulder grazing his. "How do you use one of them things? Be they complicated?"

"You but put in the powder, load the bullet...cock...aim and shoot."

She purred. "Must make you feel mighty powerful, holding such a weapon. May I try?"

She reached for the pistol, but he grasped her wrist tight enough to elicit a yelp from her.

"No one touches my pistol but me."

A little rattled, she looked at him, then to his pistol and back at him. "My, my, one would think it were made of gold."

"It be better than gold. There not be a flintlock more accurate than this one. Its range is unsurpassed for a rifle of its size. It never leaves my person."

"You sleep with it then?"

He dropped her hand and made no reply.

"I suppose if the barrel were larger, you could fuck it."

"And it wouldn't cost me a shillin' to do so."

She pursed her lips in a coquettish pout. "Then you show me. I should like to see a man such as yourself wield a weapon of death. If your other piece be as good as the pistol, mayhap it won't cost you a shillin'."

She gave him a small smile. Harry swept his gaze from her long lashes to her heaving bosom, then reached into his pocket and pulled out his pouch of powder. Holding the pistol with his hook, he opened the pouch with his hand and teeth, poured powder carefully into the barrel, then inserted a bullet.

"How about that coconut over there?" She pointed to one that had dropped onto the beach several yards away. When he did not even bother rising to his feet before cocking his pistol, she put her hand on his arm. "Wait. I can see that one is far too easy for you. How about that farther one?"

Undaunted, he rose to his feet and took aim. La Croix had stolen nearer, and was about to grab his pistol when he whipped around and pointed his firearm at her chest.

He could have shot her. No authority would have cared if one pirate killed another.

But he didn't pull the trigger—yet. He caught a rustle from the nearby bushes. Her men were moving into place to kill him should he strike, and he knew it.

"You're a dead man," La Croix said with a grin.

"So be you," Harry replied.

The end of his pistol nearly touched her bosom. She squared her shoulders as if to give him a larger target. As a blackamoor who could be sold into slavery and a pirate who was more likely to hang at Gallows Point than die in her sleep, each day she eschewed death was a surplus of time. Death was an inevitable reckoning she expected would call for her at any moment.

"Come on then," she urged in almost sultry tones. "I'll not trade my quick death for the agony of yours. My men'll carve you up like beefsteak."

She licked her lips as if anticipating a feast.

Amusement glimmered in his eyes—before a shower of glass broke over his head.

She kicked his lowered hand, knocking the pistol from him. The harlot who had smashed the bottle against his head grabbed him by the hair. He knocked her away and made for his pistol, but by then, La Croix had drawn her cutlass and a half dozen of her crew had surrounded them. Two of her men grabbed Harry and forced him to his knees while another picked up the pistol for her.

"Well done, Maggie," La Croix praised the harlot, who rubbed her rump after rising from her fall.

"Anything to avenge Olamide," Maggie replied as she wiped the sand off her skirts. "Can we kill him now?"

"In due time, *ma cherí*. I said we'd carve him up like beefsteak first."

La Croix expected the man to cower at his impending doom, but there was no distress in his eyes. Perhaps, like her, he had faced death too many times to fear it.

"Before I shoot him with the pistol that felled Olamide," she continued, taking the time to admire the firearm she held. Though not nearly as elegant as a blade, it was still a beautiful weapon, its craftsmanship evident in the scratch rifling of the barrel.

"I'm worth more to you alive than dead," said the beefsteak.

La Croix stared at the man before throwing her head back to laugh. Her men echoed her throaty guffaws.

"How be that?" she asked, wondering why she bothered asking, for there was no possible truth he could speak. Still, she was oddly curious.

"This Olamide, the man I killed," Harry continued, "I could serve you twice as well as he."

She looked him over. So the man *was* afraid, or he would not have made such an outrageous boast. She backhanded the hilt of her cutlass against the side of his face. The edge of the guard cut his cheek.

"You've no right to speak his name," she spat, retreating a step as if disgusted by the rotten stench of refuse. "Olamide served with Black Caesar. Who the hell are you?"

Though a cloud had obscured most of the moon, she could still see the whites of his eyes, bright with defiance.

"One who could be your slave."

She blinked. He didn't.

"I took your first mate," he said, "you can have me in his place."

She narrowed her eyes at him. "Why the hell would I want you in any way but dead?"

"Would it not be more fun to torture me? You could always kill me afterward."

The man was mad. No one in their right mind would invite such a death.

Or perhaps he did not fully appreciate who she was.

"Lift him to his feet," she commanded.

Her men did as told. She covered the distance between her and her quarry, slowly, as if approaching a lover. She gazed up at him, at the blood trickling from his cut...

Then swiftly brought her knee into his groin.

He would have doubled over, but her men held him in place as she struck him several more times with her knee.

"Drop him," she ordered.

Without support, he collapsed onto hands and knees. She kicked him in the ribs, then his jaw. He bit the beach and coughed on the sand. She pointed his pistol at him.

"Still want to be my slave, *joli garçon*?"

Suppressing a grimace, he found her gaze through the dark. He spit sand and blood out the side of his mouth. "Aye. I do."

He spoke as if taking a marital vow. She felt the muscle beneath her right eye twitch. A white man was offering himself as a slave to a negress? Such a thing did not exist in the West Indies.

She had never thought to own a slave. As a child, she and her mother were the slaves. Baron La Croix had sold her mother to a plantation owner in Kingston. He had not known at the time that she was with his child, but La Croix doubted that would have stopped him. Several years later, the baron had passed through Kingston and decided to buy back his former slave, as well as the child.

"Kill him already," Maggie spat. "He ain't too pretty to die."

But La Croix had uncocked the pistol. The man was right. She need not be in a hurry to kill him.

And that was how Harry had come aboard the

Bloody Baron.

CHAPTER THREE

~ 1714, Nassau ~

L a Croix had not expected to let Harry live as long as she did. And never would she have thought to allow him between her legs.

Because she didn't fuck men.

But Harry had shown surprising fortitude, though she had done her best to wring dry his will to live. First, she'd had him locked in a cell in the bowels of the ship, leaving him to wonder for days how and when he would die. On the seventh day, she had ordered him to be brought above deck. Not having seen the sun in a sennight, he could not open his eyes for some time. He had been fed only rancid water and moldy bread that even the weevils did not want, but though thinner, he still possessed an admirable form. His breeches still molded rugged thighs, and he had not lost all the muscles in his arms.

Over time, as she made him take on the most arduous tasks aboard ship, his arms and legs had regained their supple bulges. And through the most menial, the most grotesque duties, Harry had never complained, nor ever so much as winced. Still, every day she had toyed with the thought of killing him.

Until they fucked for the first time.

In the private chambers of a brothel, a beautiful redhead thrust her hips at La Croix, causing the feeble bed to thump loudly against the wall.

"Harder, *ma cheri*, harder," La Croix ordered the harlot riding atop her as she lay upon her back. She needed the release, to let the tension and anger at losing one of her sloops and a third of her crew.

The *Bloody Baron* had come across an East Indiaman, a prize beyond compare, laden with riches from the Orient. Delacroix, who had succeeded Olamide as her first mate, captaining a sloop that she had captured from another pirate, was supposed to stay back, for they had sighted a British third rate roaming the waters a few days ago.

But instead of defending the *Baron* when a naval ship, which had lain in hiding behind a small peninsula, nearly blew a hole into the side of the *Baron*, Delacroix had chosen to flee rather than exchange gunfire. Luckily for the *Baron*, the third rate went after Delacroix, perhaps thinking the sloop the superior. After exchanging cannonfire with the East Indiaman, La Croix was forced to retreat when the third rate changed its mind and returned to protect the East Indiaman.

La Croix grunted. Her body felt as if it were coiled tighter than a spring, and if she did not spend soon, she might implode. She had not even bothered to remove her garments, which would have made the heat from their exertions insufferable but for a greater corporal urgency. Upon entering the chambers, she had pulled the redhead to her, smothered her lips with a kiss, and dragged her to the bed.

The dildo strapped to the harlot penetrated deep but did not always strike where needed. La Croix regretted not having disrobed the wench, whose motions were perhaps hampered by the layers of petticoats bunched at her waist. La Croix pumped her own hips and managed to find a better angle.

"A little faster," La Croix encouraged, feeling the pleasure finally beginning to crescendo. She moaned as her lashes fluttered. "*Oui. Oui.*"

Just then the door to the chamber flew open.

La Croix widened her eyes to see the flash of a knife above her. When the harlot turned around in surprise, La Croix toppled her off the bed and grabbed her cutlass from its sheath. Hopping off the bed, she planted her boot upon the knife before the harlot could reach it.

"I saw the knife behind her back," Harry explained of his intrusion. He stood near with a pistol pointed at the wench, who shrank from the cutlass before her and crouched in the corner.

La Croix eyed the terrified young woman whom she had lain with a few times before. "You meant to kill me, *ma cheri*?"

Red tendrils fell across her face as she shook her head. "Nay, I—"

She shrieked when La Croix shoved the cutlass closer to her.

"It was Vane!" the harlot cried. "He promised me a hundred pieces of eight if I maimed or killed you."

"Charles Vane?" Harry echoed.

"He once attempted to turn my men against me," La Croix explained, "so I set fire to one of his boats."

"P-Please don't kill me," the wench begged, with tears glistening down the sides of her face.

"Now, *ma cherí*, how can I let you live after what you tried?"

Her face fell and her body shook.

"The doxy might prove a better deterrent if she lived," Harry offered.

La Croix glared at his nonsense.

"Her death would be forgot within days," he said. "But alive, she would be a walking reminder of what might happen to those who think to profit from harming you."

Curious, La Croix allowed him to continue. Harry uncocked his pistol and returned it to his belt. Approaching the harlot, he grasped her jaw. She clawed at him but could not dislodge his tight grasp. With his hook, he began to carve into her cheek.

Her shrieks split the air. Eyes wide with panic, she struggled and kicked at him.

"Be still, love," Harry said, "or I might nick

your eye."

When he was done, her left cheek bore a bloody "L" while her right sported the letter "C."

Impressed, La Croix sheathed her cutlass. "On your way then, *ma cherí*, before I change my mind about killing you."

Harry released the sobbing woman, who tripped on her skirts several times before scrambling away.

"The scars should last a few years, mayhap more," Harry said after she had left. Taking out a handkerchief, he wiped the blood from his hook.

La Croix thought of the scars she had imposed upon his back. Why had he not let the wench kill her? Given all that Harry had suffered at her hands, if she had been in his boots, she would not have chosen to save her captain. Indeed, she would have ensured death with the pistol he held. A pistol she had not provided.

But the agitation swirling in her loins recalled her to the cravings that had been left unsated. Though she was grateful for Harry's intervention, the evening had not ended as she had wished.

"Kneel," she ordered him.

Though taken aback, he did as told. With his

height, his head came level to her chest, the perfect height for what she wanted to do.

"You say you saw the knife at her back?" she asked.

"The door was ajar."

"You were watching us. For how long?"

"But a minute or two."

"You could have let her kill me."

"Aye."

"Why did you not?"

"You're my captain."

She weighed his answers as she searched his countenance for elements of prevarication. Seeing none, she drove her fist into the side of his face.

"What the bloody—what was that for?" he demanded when he had recovered from the blow.

"For watching."

Her unbuttoned breeches hung upon her hips, and she drew them up with a sigh of vexation. Her climb up rapture's walls had been interrupted by a slut's greed. She would have to tend to her own needs, for she was too impatient to go in search of another wench. And they would not likely wish to lie with her after seeing her initials bleeding on the face of one of their own.

Harry stared at her groin. "Let a real cock pleasure you."

La Croix wrinkled her nose. "Fucking a man be more trouble than it's worth."

"Then you've not been properly fucked."

She snorted. How many times at sea had she eyed one of her crew and wished that she could ride him? Carnal urges coursed as strong through her as any of their sex. But she did not trust men.

"I can lick your cunnie as well as that doxy," Harry added.

She leveled her fist at him again, silently swearing to herself, for the impact hurt her knuckles as much as it might have hurt him.

"You were watching for more than a minute or two," she accused.

After working his jaw, he returned his head to meet her gaze. She thought his eyes would blaze with outrage, but only the glimmer of lust was for certain.

"Your pardon," he said with icy calm.

She threaded her fingers into his hair and yanked his head back. "Did it arouse you to be peeping?"

"If you had invited me in, it would have been

a privilege greater than the entry to heaven," he replied with a hint of mockery, but also the edge of truth. It intrigued her.

She pulled out her dagger and put the tip to his throat. "I never granted you a pistol. How did you come by one?"

"From our raid on Cayo Santa Maria."

That had been a few months ago. He had a pistol in his possession all this time?

"Why hadn't you killed me yet?"

Her mind whirled, trying to recall if he might have made any attempts. He had not wanted for opportunities, for a year into his servitude, she had begun to give him liberties till he walked as free as the rest of her crew.

He knew that if he had harmed her, there were those among her crew who would have killed him in gruesome fashion, and perhaps that had stayed his hand, but she would not have been surprised if he was willing to take that chance. He did not fear death as most men did. She could not decide if it was fearlessness, recklessness, arrogance, or stupidity.

Or, perhaps, it was because he was in some manner dead already.

"Why?" she demanded with a forceful tug upon his hair.

"Because I'd rather fuck you."

Lust had thawed the ice in his eyes. Glancing down, she saw the bulge at his crotch. She clenched her thighs at her own craving.

"You would, eh?"

She needed no response beyond the flare of his nostrils. The tension between her legs made itself known.

"I'll let you pleasure me," she acquiesced, "but if you should disappoint, I might be tempted to kill you."

She did not reveal that he would be the first man to lay an intimate hand upon her body in nearly ten years. Reaching down, she removed his sword and pistol and tossed them aside. Her gaze trailed down his naked arms, for he wore a sleeveless shirt beneath his waistcoat. She licked her bottom lip. Excitement boiled inside her at what she was about to permit.

"Arms behind your back," she ordered, then undid the sash from her hips to bind his wrists. Still holding the dagger, she pressed the blade to the side of his neck as she leaned in. "Speak a word of this, and I'll maroon you without a pistol."

The scent of his unwashed body, his perspiration from the dampness of summer, his masculinity, did not repulse her as the stench of some men did. Her head throbbed in warning, but the heat of desire spoke louder. She would but let him taste her a little, she reasoned. He was hers to command, after all.

Straightening before him, she pushed her breeches down past her hips, revealing her womanhood. He perked, like a wolf scenting raw meat, and stared at the mossy curls adorning her pelvis.

"Feast then, slave."

Still on his knees, he inched forward to her, sank onto his haunches and buried his face between her legs. He knew to target the clitoris. Despite the ravenous look in his eyes, he drew himself languidly over the nub. The texture of his tongue made her shiver, and she nearly dropped her dagger.

He had a larger tongue than the redhead but maneuvered it with skillful delicacy. *Merde!* Did he practice this form, like a painter or sculptor perfecting his art? Looking down, she watched her curls brush over his nose as the tip of his tongue toyed with her.

Her legs trembled when he drew the width of his tongue along her flesh. She wondered how many women he had lain with? With his comely countenance, there would be no shortage of the fair sex willing to lift their skirts beneath him, despite their low numbers in the West Indies.

A strange seed of jealousy sprouted. Harry was hers. Her slave.

He flicked his tongue lightly over her pleasure nub, and a soft moan escaped her lips. Bracing herself against the foot of the bed, she parted her legs farther and angled her pelvis to give him greater access. A delicious heat wrapped her loins, and with a tight grip about her dagger, she allowed her eyes to close. She gasped when his tongue found a sensitive spot, which he proceeded to tease and caress with vigilance.

His application kicked up a storm inside her. Her body succumbed to a most delightful paroxysm. Her hips bucked against him. Once more she nearly dropped her dagger.

His appetite seemed to surge, and he lapped at her voraciously until the sensations were too much for her to bear. She yanked his head back by his hair. Her wetness glistened upon his face. His perseverance impressed her, for she did not spend easily. The gleam in his eyes suggested he could have continued for longer.

"Not done yet, are we?" he inquired.

She raised her brows. Did he know how often she liked to spend? Had he peeped in on her before? Or did he speak in hopes that he could taste of satisfaction?

"My cock is yours to use as you will," he enticed.

A glutton for spending, she welcomed a second course. Curious to see what his shaft looked like, she pushed him down. He landed on his back upon the wooden floorboards. Hovering over him, she sliced open his fall. He muffled a curse, for now he would have to find a way to mend his breeches.

A beautiful pole protruded from his pelvis. Unlike the dildo the harlot had used, his erection had a subtle curve. La Croix straightened and felt the lust flare to her head. To have such a rugged man bound and at her mercy was intoxicating. She wrapped her free hand about his member, felt it pulse beneath her fingers. Her wetness grew.

Still, she had never had a real cock inside her. Would it feel much different than a dildo?

"Are you afraid to use it?"

She narrowed her eyes at him, not liking the taunt. She cupped his cods and squeezed them harshly. He choked down a howl. Satisfied that he would not challenge her again, she rose, pulled up her breeches, and went in search of a condom.

"You won't need one," he said. "You'll spend afore me."

She looked in the drawers of the sideboard. "Ha! Your sex—and your kind in particular—are not likely to last more than ten minutes."

Which was another reason she did not trouble to lie with men. They lacked endurance.

"Care to lay a wager on it?" Harry asked.

Take aback by his arrogance, she returned to stand over him. She put her hands upon her hips. "What manner of wager?"

"If I spend first—"

"If you spill your seed in me, I slice your throat."

The thought of becoming with child made her shiver in disgust, but there was an old witch woman on the island who claimed to sell a brew that could induce an abortion.

"But if you spend first, you release me from my bondage."

"You want your freedom?"

"And my pistol back."

She considered his proposition. His precious pistol lay in a box in her cabin, waiting for the day she decided to end his life. But she had enjoyed torturing Harry and, of late, no longer desired to kill him. He had proven himself a valuable member of the crew, equal to her best.

Could he really outlast her? With his freedom as enticement, he had every reason to try. But either way, she would lose him. He would be free or he would be dead.

Nonplussed, she shook her head. If freedom was what he sought, he would have gained it sooner had he allowed the redhead to kill her, or shot her himself with the pistol he had kept secret all this time.

"And why would I take such a wager?" La Croix asked. "The prize be good for you, but what be in it for me?"

"Aside from the chance to kill me?"

"I could kill you now if I wanted to."

He paused in thought. "How about ten thousand pieces of eight?"

He had her attention. "What ten thousand pieces of eight?"

"Four years ago, I took a Spanish galleon carrying eighty thousand reales. It was why Chacón sliced off my hand. I had refused to reveal where I'd hid the treasure."

"*C'est des conneries.* You've no treasure."

"But what if I did?"

To her surprise, her cunnie pulsed. She recalled how delectably his tongue had caressed her. His erection, still standing tall, beckoned. She needed a fuck. The harlot's dildo was nowhere to be seen. Perhaps it was still upon the wench.

La Croix held her dagger and inspected the blade to ensure it was sharp enough to saw off a man's cock. "Why did you not offer these pieces of eight before?"

"Because I was sure you wanted to kill me more than you wanted the silver."

"And you think today be different somehow?"

He eyed her dagger. "My cock performs better when it is attached to me."

She started at how he had read her mind, though it was not the first time he had anticipated her. On a number of occasions, he had guessed what she had expected of him. There was the time he had finished swabbing bilge water before she had given him the order to do so. And readied a torch before she had threatened to set fire to an American vessel carrying slaves to Virginia.

Her mouth watered as her gaze went to his cock once more. If she spent first, she would forego a fine crewmember and an even finer slave. If he spent first, she would take his silver, then kill him. She wanted the silver, provided he spoke truthfully. But she wanted to spend again.

Which did she want more?

CHAPTER FOUR

"You've a mighty fine opinion of your cock," she sneered. Perhaps she could sample it before she decided whether or not to accept his wager.

"Have a taste," he invited.

She nearly threw herself at him. Instead, she forced herself to be patient and kicked off her boots, wanting to give only indications of her command and forbearance. She slid down her breeches, satisfied to see the hunger swell in his eyes. She had long hairless legs, legs that filled the length of a man's breeches. Only her hips and arse made the breeches fit a little too tight. Setting aside her dagger, she removed her coat, though it did little to ease the fire raging within her, but it did give her time to think. She wanted both the silver and to spend. Surely there was a way to achieve both.

She shed her waistcoat but kept her shirt. No

man had seen her fully naked before.

Dagger back in hand, she sank to her knees and touched the blade to his cock. "It be a pretty pole, to be sure. Shame if I had to cut it off."

"At least use it a few times before you do."

The hoarseness in his voice made her pulse quicken. She straddled his hips and ground herself upon his pelvis, coating him with her wetness. Pleasure blossomed where flesh met flesh. She used the base of his cock to rub her clitoris, purring at the delightful friction.

She had an inspiration: she would make him spend first, then, as he was still her slave, she would make him fuck her on pain of death, but without the reward of freedom.

"I accept your wager, slave."

Lifting herself up, she sank down on his shaft and caught the sound of a growl low in his throat.

He felt glorious. Much finer than the dildo. Like velvet-covered flint. After savoring how he filled her, how he seemed to touch her in places the dildo could not, she rolled her hips, exploring all angles of exquisiteness.

She had not realized she had closed her eyes until she opened them to find Harry staring at her, his eyes bright with arousal. He throbbed inside of her, and her ravenous cunnie clenched in response. Remembering her intentions, she began to slide up and down his rod, doing her best to graze her clitoris against him whenever she came down. He began bucking his hips in rhythm to hers, spearing himself deeper into her.

She should disengage before one of them spent. She wanted him to spend first, but she did not want his seed inside her womb. Yet she found it hard to tear herself from the rapture building betwixt them. Perhaps another minute...

He slammed his hips up into her. Pleasure and pain lanced through her. The dagger clattered to the floor. She wanted more, her cunnie screaming in protest when she came off his cock. Every muscle in her body tensed, but the sooner she made him spend, the sooner she could reap the rewards.

Kneeling between his spread legs, she gripped his cock and fitted her mouth over its tip, tasting her own arousal. He let out an oath. This was what men enjoyed most, more than cunnie even. Though she had never swallowed cock before, she had seen enough whores do it. She tasted her own wetness and a tang that was his. She engulfed more of him and triumphed at his groan. She bobbed her head up and down, sometimes teasing him by remaining at the tip before sinking to take more of him into her mouth. The area between her legs pulsed in jealousy. She stroked herself with her free hand to address the deficit. Shivers went down his legs as she intensified her feasting.

"Bloody hell," he cursed when he realized that he was doomed to lose the wager.

If her mouth were not stuffed with cock, she would have smiled to herself. That should put his bravado in its place. She sucked on his cock as hard as she could while quickening the hand between her thighs. She sank two fingers into her cunnie, but the digits felt paltry. She hoped he would spend soon. If she should discover that the pieces of eight did not exist, she would cut every inch of him and hang him up by his toes before she made him a eunuch.

Suddenly, she was thrown onto her back against the floor, her body pinned beneath Harry, the blade of her dagger resting against the side of her neck.

Too late, she realized she ought to have

restrained him more. Would he kill her now?

"My freedom and my pistol if you spend first," he reminded her.

Her eyes blazed with anger. Not bloody likely.

But he refuted her resolve when he slapped his member against her flesh. He prodded her with his tip but did not enter. She did not know if she was more furious at him or at the betrayal of her own body. She lay still, unsure if he would slice her if she struggled. But he did not mean to kill her. Not yet. Not till he had proved his point

The head of his cock burrowed into her folds, making her whimper. He allowed an inch, then two, to slip in. Her breath caught, and her cunnie clamped greedily at the offering, wanting more. He reached between her thighs with his free hand and found her clitoris. Her eyes rolled toward the back of her head. *Aie pitié.*

For several minutes he fondled her clitoris, till her hips moved of their own accord, inviting more of him inside. He obliged and pushed the rest of his length into her, till the curls at his base entwined with hers. She trembled, tried to resist the tension that must need worsen before it could improve. Gradually he began thrusting, long, languid strokes that made her want to scale the walls. But even as her body gloried in the assault, her mind protested.

She did not want to spend. She did not want to be wrong and Harry to be right. She wanted him as her slave still, so that she could punish him for the pleasure he presently forced upon her.

As if sensing her hesitation, he withdrew both his cock and his thumb. Her cunnie gaped at the loss. Her clitoris tingled.

"Did you not want to spend?"

She glared at him, willing him to see the torment she would put him through if she survived. She choked down a cry of anguish. If the tension inside her was not allowed to burst, she feared her body would wither.

"Fuck me," she commanded.

"Aye, aye, Captain."

With a swift thrust, he buried himself in her wet heat. He rolled his hips, and each wave of pleasure was greater than the last, till she was crushed beneath, her body shaking into pieces, a silent scream upon her lips. Liquid sprayed from between her legs, soaking into the wood below. He pulled out and plunged back in several times to wring the last of the spasms from her cunnie. He grunted with each spray of wetness, and she found her voice, alternating between groaning and screaming.

When she could do no more than lay and shudder, he sat back on his haunches, jerked his cock furiously and spent with a roar that filled the room. He doubled over as if kicked in the stomach as his seed spilled, a few drops landing upon her thigh. He collapsed against the end of the bed, his head resting over the edge.

For several minutes, La Croix stared at the rafters above, waiting for the errant throbbing in her body to quiet.

Harry was right: she had never been properly fucked before. If she had known such euphoria was possible, she would have ordered Harry to fuck her long ago.

But he was no longer hers to command. She had spent first. Fate was indeed a cruel mistress.

"Give me my bloody dagger," she barked as she sat up and took it from him.

Harry handed her his handkerchief after she had risen to her feet. She shook her head. What manner of pirate kept a handkerchief? But she accepted the article, stained with the harlot's blood, and wiped the wetness about her thighs. She grabbed her breeches and slid them on.

"Your pistol be aboard ship," she told him.

"It'll be good to have her back."

He rose to his feet and stared at his open fall. She smirked. Now that he had his freedom, he should not allow a minor inconvenience to trouble him. But her mood had improved from spending—magnificently. She felt in generous spirits.

"I'll see if one of the wenches has needle and thread," she offered, tying the dagger to her thigh before departing.

"Captain," he said, sitting himself upon the edge of the bed. "Is the *Bloody Baron* not in need of a first mate?"

She turned to face him. In her mind, she had decided to make her boatswain her new first mate. But when she looked into Harry's eyes, still molten and no longer unsettling, she realized who her first mate would actually be. Her heart did an odd skip at the prospect of retaining Harry.

Alas, he would no longer be her slave, but he had become something better. And she could still impose upon him as his captain.

"I'll think on it," she replied, but he knew her decision, for one corner of his mouth had curled. She stared at his lips, wondering what it would feel like to be kissed by them.

She took a step toward him instead of the door. He raised his brows but seemed to recognize her thoughts. The needle and thread could wait.

CHAPTER FIVE

Perhaps she should have gone for the needle and thread as she had intended and given her arousal time to cool. She cursed her body and its carnal appetite. Once it had blossomed, feeding her lust seemed to only make it hungrier. She could not deny that his sex had a strength that no doxy could match. Nevertheless, she had not expected to enjoy tumbling Harry as much as she had.

After delaying her search for needle and thread, she had turned to face him. He half-sat, half-leaned against the bed, his muscular frame making the bed appear small. His fall lay open, but he almost seemed to welcome her stare of his now flaccid cock. She had thought her body done, but it wanted another taste of him.

Should she reveal her desires to him? He seemed to sense it in the way that he returned her stare. As captain, she should make the first move, but what if he thought he now held an advantage? He was likely to know that she did not lay with men. The few sailors who had not been enlightened to this and dared ogle, flirt, offer a bawdy remark, or attempt any form of seduction with her had been promptly kicked off the crew.

The air betwixt her and Harry had thickened with tension as neither made a move. She saw his cock harden and was impressed at its ready return.

"Come hither," she ordered for no purpose other than to assert her command. Though no longer in servitude to her, she would only consider him for first mate if he obeyed.

Standing, he strode wordlessly to her. He stood mere inches away and seemed taller now that he was no longer her slave.

"What is it you desire, Captain?" he asked gently. His cock had risen and lengthened.

"If you can make me spend a third time, I might consider you for first mate."

"You'll want to consider me regardless."

She raised her brows at his bold declaration. "An' you fail, I want a share of your pieces of eight."

"If I fail, you can have all my pieces of eight."

"Ha! These pieces of eight do not exist if you are so willing to part with them."

She still failed to see how, if he indeed possessed this treasure, he would wish to trouble himself with piracy or settle for being her first mate when he could captain his own crew if he truly enjoyed being a pirate.

"The pieces of eight are real," he replied, "but I don't aim to fail."

She had drawn in a quick breath before scoffing. "On with it, then."

He had yanked her to him. She collided into his hard chest. His mouth descended upon hers, his lips crushing and bruising. Her mind swam from the force of his kiss. She had never before been kissed so hard. It differed from the gentle, soft kisses of the whores she had bedded. Unaccustomed to having her mouth smothered, she sought space and room to breathe, but his hand was at the back of her head, holding her in place as he devoured her. She reached for the dagger at her thigh, but just as suddenly, he lightened the kiss. His hook was beneath her jaw, tilting her chin up as he tasted of her upper lip, tugged at her bottom lip, and parted them both for the entry of his tongue. Her whole body shivered.

A warning bell sounded. Her head was trapped. With his strength, he could break her neck. She drew the dagger, though she knew, at best, she could only maim him if her death was not instantaneous. It would not be wise to continue. She should wrest herself free and make him lick her cunnie again, in a position that gave her the advantage.

But as he continued to probe the depths of her mouth, the heat from his melding with hers, her hot breath bouncing off him back into her own face, she could not bring herself to tear away. She was dancing with danger, but fear only fueled her ardor. Lust rose from her loins to her head like smoke, clouding her judgment.

Not wanting to submit to his imposition, she decided to kiss him back. She shoved her hips at him. He was not without hunger for her—she could feel his hardness pressing into her—and if he had thoughts of harming her, he might wish to wait until he had satiated himself first.

Eager to be the aggressor, she shoved her

mouth into his whilst he was exploring hers with reverential caresses. She knew no art with kissing, unlike Harry, who demonstrated more refinement and precision, skills perhaps acquired from kissing ladies of elegance. Her kisses, by comparison, were careless, undirected, and not unlike the sloppy slathering she once received from a mongrel her father had refused to allow her to keep.

She sucked his upper lip and bit his lower lip, pushing her tongue into him so indiscriminately that she licked his teeth half the time. He met her offensive and, accepting the dance, returned her ferocity. Circling an arm about her, he whirled her about till her back landed against the wall. Her dagger clattered to the floor. She was trapped between two planes of hardness, though she found relief that he no longer held her head. She entwined her fingers into his hair, pulling and twisting till he grunted. Their tongues dueled. As if wielding swords, they thrust and parried. Her jaw grew sore, and she felt she was losing the battle. He was bigger, stronger, and more practiced. She panted, as if she had scaled the rigging to the mainmast.

She needed to catch her breath. As if granting her a reprieve, or because he knew she had conceded, he moved his mouth off hers. His lips traced her jaw till he reached her ear. She gasped, having never been kissed there. He proceeded down her throat, taking hot, wet mouthfuls. Wetness pooled in her breeches, the moisture unable to douse the lust blazing through the whole of her body. She wrapped her legs about him and ground herself into his groin. He grabbed her left thigh and bucked his hips as if his cock could pierce through her breeches. Though each thrust slammed her against the wall, she thrilled to the motion. Such a position were not possible with a woman.

He rubbed his erection against her crotch till she could stand it no more. She fumbled with the buttons of her fall. He wasted no time and speared himself into her wet heat. No drink could quench her thirst as well as his stiff cock. Her cunnie pulsed and flexed about the member. Using the wall behind her as leverage, she was able to roll her hips. He followed her rhythm and together they coaxed the waves of rapture higher and higher.

Before she could reach the pinnacle, however, he slowed his thrusting.

"Not yet," he grumbled into her ear.

Not yet? What the bloody hell did he mean by that? The position had taxed her muscles, and the exertion had her breathing hard. This delay would cost him. She was about to say as much when he pulled her from the wall and carried her to the bed. He laid her down, undid the last of her buttons and pulled her breeches down her hips. The scent of her arousal wafted through the air. His nostrils flared. He brushed the damp curls at her mons. She gave a huff of impatience, then her breath stalled when he moved his hook between her legs. With the back of the hook, he nudged the rosebud between her folds. The steel felt cool against her hot flesh. The last thing she should want between her legs was something sharp, but once more fear taunted her arousal to new heights. She let out a shaky breath as the arc of his hook stroked her and nudged the nub of pleasure from side to side. As he fondled her, he seemed to drink in every moan. The tension in her loins mounted, and she was almost inclined to hump his hook, but to her irritation, he withdrew. Had he forgotten his pieces at eight were at stake?

Sitting up, she grabbed his shirtfront and yanked him toward her. She snarled, "What game do you play?"

"Trust me," he answered, his face mere inches from her, his breath slightly uneven. "Your patience shall see its reward."

"Damn your patience."

"Delaying the climax enhances its glory."

She had never heard such shite. Surely constant denial would only lead to sufferance or even boredom.

"I want to spend *now*, not bloody later."

As she glared at him and saw the lust glowing in his eyes, she wondered that he could hold back. Here was willing cunnie to be had. While he knew better than to spill his seed inside her, the sooner he saw her spend, the sooner he could attend to himself.

"Does rum not taste sweeter when there is none to be had?" he returned.

She narrowed her eyes, suspicious of his motives. Why did he risk her ire?

"I don't give a shite about rum, Harry."

She rarely called him by name, and he seemed

amused to hear it.

"You don't believe me," he commented.

She snorted. "You think I prefer whores who are slow and try my patience?"

"I think there is much to fucking you've not tried."

Perturbed and curious all at once, she offered no response. How much more to fucking could there be?

He lowered his voice. "Trust me."

"Trust you? And why should I trust a bloody Englishman?"

"You trust me enough to make me first mate."

"I said I would think on it."

"I haven't killed you yet, have I?" He lay his hook beside her neck. "It would have been so easy to boot."

Save for a few quick blinks, she refused to evince any fear before him. Her dagger and cutlass lay painfully far from her. But he had had more than one opportunity to hurt her tonight. She still wondered why he had not.

His hook traced her jawline, and she caught a whiff of her own musk upon the metal.

"It better be as good as you say," she relented.

Without word, he pulled off her boots before stripping off her breeches. He brushed his hand along the length of one bare leg. She rolled her eyes in exasperation. Such fineries might suit for bedding a gentlewoman, but she wanted not soft caresses. She wanted hard cock.

"I've not felt such silken legs before," he murmured, "as smooth as the skin of babes."

She spread her legs. He grinned at the obvious invitation. He ran his hand along her inner thigh to the crook where her leg joined her pelvis before continuing to her mound. He inserted two fingers into her cunnie.

That was much better. Her cunnie grasped at the welcome intrusion. Though she preferred cock, she would gladly fuck his hand. All previous tension returned to seek that euphoric release.

His fingers curled, stroking the underside of her lower belly.

"*Mon dieu*," she breathed. She almost laughed with joy at the pleasure reverberating inside her. "*Oui...encore...*"

He stroked her with a little more intensity. The most beautiful sensations rioted within her.

"*Oui, mon dieu, oui.*"

Her arousal ascended toward that divine end, and, just as before, he withdrew before she could round the pinnacle. Her body screamed in protest as she lay there, as if she had had the wind knocked from her.

With a roar, she scrambled up, pounced on him and shoved him onto his back. He allowed her this for she would not otherwise have been able to pin him to the bed. If her desire to fuck were not superior, she would have wanted to beat him to a bloody pulp. Grabbing his erection, she sank herself down his length. She closed her eyes and relished the hardness within her. His cock felt more exquisite than before—a sweeter rum.

She ground her pelvis into him, but he grabbed her hips, limiting the force of her motions. She choked on a howl, feeling his hook pressed against her right hip bone. When she had the chance, she was going to kill him.

He flexed his cock inside her, making her shiver, before rolling her hips over him in slow, measured motions. She wanted to ride his cock roughly and with fury, but the pleasant sensations rippling through her lower body were enough to stay her desire to harm him. Still chasing the climax she had been denied, she tried to push herself down harder, but he controlled the pace and pressure.

"Patience, Captain," he urged.

If she could hurt him with her glare, she would. Granted, the journey to lust's end was delicious as he dragged her up the length of his shaft and rolled her down, but she had not the patience to savor it.

"*Mon dieu*, even Bridgette can fuck harder than you," she spat. Bridgette was a whore in Kingston and a dwarf. The men thought it amusing to fuck a woman half their size. Some thought her cunnie, being significantly smaller, would be tighter.

Harry only grinned. He circled his hook about the back of her slender neck and pulled her down to him, crushing her lips to his. With his hook about the most vulnerable part of her body, she dared not move, allowing him to maul her mouth. Her lips hurt from the bruising, and she supposed she merited the response for her words.

Despite the discomfort of having her bent legs cramped beneath her and fearing that any rash movement would get her nicked by his hook, arousal coursed as potent as ever through her.

As long as she remained impaled upon his cock she would endure any pain and discomfort. He devoured her every breath, making her head spin from want of air, but when he released her mouth, the relief seemed to go straight to her belly, causing the flames there to surge.

"You've such fine lips, Captain," he said, brushing a thumb over her bottom lip.

She was aware that her lips were thicker than most women's. At the moment, her lips felt swollen to twice their size. Nevertheless, she needed no compliments from him.

She cursed him, "*Va te faire foutre.*"

Harry spoke no French, but he seemed to know her words. "As you wish."

He bucked his hips, and she felt the point of his hook dig into her shoulder when her body slid up his. If he drew blood, she would take ten drops for each one that spilled from her. She decided against speaking her thoughts. She could not fully trust that he would do her no harm. In all her past dealings with him, she had always been in command. At present, it did not feel so.

Holding her in place, he drew his cock in and

out of her at a languid pace. She moaned, her lashes fluttering. Her body was on edge, and it would not likely take much to make her spend. Her womb tightened, her cunnie clenched. He slowed his motions. She whimpered. Glory had been within her reach! She nearly begged him to continue, but she had never begged for anything of anyone. As she lay there, her cunnie pulsing at the ready, she knew not what to do. Taunts and threats had availed her naught. What had she gotten herself into?

Gradually, the movement of his hips returned. She could have cried with delight. This time, his cock stroked her until she finally found release, the longest, deepest release she had ever known. She wailed as wave after wave of euphoria passed through her, leaving her body a mass of trembling nerves.

He pushed her off his chest, and though she wanted to collapse, she remained erect. Grabbing her hips, he slammed his hips up. His hardness lanced through her. If not for her state of rapture, she would have found his pounding near painful. It made her teeth chatter. But when he paused to fondle her clitoris, a second paroxysm erupted within her. Her cries turned silent as the intensity threatened to shatter her body into pieces.

With a feral grunt, he grabbed her hips and speared himself into her several times before tossing her from her perch. His back arched, his muscles tensed, and his legs quivered as his seed shot forth. His body shook as he milked the last drop with his hand, then he sank into the bed with a haggard exhale.

"What was it you said of Bridgette now?" he asked between strong breaths.

Still recovering, she made no reply at first.

"That you be a better fuck than she."

"I thought that be what you said. It would wound my pride much to think I could not best a midget."

She snickered and decided not to reveal the fact that she had never lain with Bridgette, whose size and tiny voice reminded La Croix too much of a child. She knew not in the least how the whore fucked.

CHAPTER SIX

"Poirier will piss himself when he learns he'll not be first mate," La Croix reflected as she stared up at the ceiling. She lay in bed, her body satiated after having ridden Harry for a good thirty minutes.

"Aye, that he will," Harry, lying beside her, agreed with indifference. "He'll shite himself, too, knowin' that the first mate be an Englishman."

She stretched her legs, half surprised herself. Before Harry, she would never have thought to appoint an Englishman to any post of importance aboard her ship. She hated the English.

"You better not give me cause to hang you from the yardarm," she spat, reconsidering her decision. Her crew comprised many a Frenchman who had sailed under her father, and not one of them cared for the English, though she was aware that Harry had managed to earn the grudging respect of many in her crew. Harry was not afraid to be the first to board an enemy ship, put himself in the way of danger to aid a crewmember, or run into gunfire as if to taunt Death. If the men did not respect him, they feared him to be mad. Harry had once taken on a crewmember twice his size. Bludgeoned and bleeding, Harry had yet managed to knock the giant unconscious. La Croix had punished them both for fighting aboard ship, sentencing them to twenty lashes each before being clapped in irons.

"It be sporting of you to give an Englishman a chance," Harry said.

She snorted. "I pray your kind be good for something."

He turned to stare at her, his smoldering gaze making her breath hitch. She knew his thoughts, and they nettled her.

"Don't give yourself airs," she responded. "You ain't the best fuck I've ever had. Black cock be better—and bigger."

A muscle rippled along his jaw, and she wondered if he might be jealous.

"Don't believe me?" she asked before he could ask anything of her.

"I don't disagree, Captain."

70

She raised a brow, idly wondering if he had buggered or been buggered before. To her surprise, she found the musing provocative.

"My first time at sea, I sailed with a blackamoor," Harry informed, "a former slave who had escaped from Antigua. Blaggard had the most monstrous cock I ever saw. In its erect state, it appeared as long as his forearm."

She glanced down at her own forearm, wondering if she could take a cock its length. She shivered.

"But if you didn't think my cock half-decent," Harry continued, "you wouldn't have spread your legs atop me."

Her mind flashed to how she had straddled his hips upon the bed and ground herself into him, smashing her clit into his pubis. As a result of her exertions, her garments—she had removed only her breeches—now clung to her, damp from perspiration. She glanced at where his fall only partially covered his former glory.

"Consider yourself a lucky *salaud*," she spat, "to have been present when I was feeling randy. An Englishman would otherwise be my last choice for a tumble."

She sat up to reach for her breeches, ready to be done with his company.

"And why be that, may I ask?"

She paused. In truth, the Spanish were as bad as the English, and the French little better. Though she had French blood in her veins, her kind had no allegiances, no loyalties to the nations that had enslaved them.

"After begetting my mother with child, my father sold her to an Englishman in Kingston," she answered.

"Is that how you came to speak English?"

"I learned the language so that I could curse him to his face one day."

"Your master or your father?"

She could not help a small grin at his insight. "I curse them both: the Baron in French, and the slaveowner in English."

For emphasis, she expectorated onto the floor before pulling up her breeches.

"The Baron sailed under L'Ollonais," Harry said.

"*Oui.* In his early years as a buccaneer."

"Was L'Ollonais as cruel as they say?"

"The Baron challenged us to find anyone more

vicious. My father told of how, when being led by two prisoners L'Ollonais took at the port of Puerto Caballos, they broke through a Spanish ambush en route to San Pedro. Enraged, L'Ollonais ripped through one of the prisoners with his cutlass, tore out the beating heart and gnawed it before casting it into the face of the other prisoner."

She watched Harry eye his hook and wondered how often he had sliced a man with it. The precision with which he had cut the whore had been impressive.

"Was your father with him till the end?"

"There were no spoils to be had at San Pedro, which L'Ollonais burned. The Baron deserted then with one of the smaller boats. It was not long after that L'Ollonais sailed to the Gulf of Darien and was captured by cannibals."

"And hacked to pieces before being roasted limb by limb. Or so the tale goes."

La Croix grunted. She had heard the stories of L'Ollonais a hundred times.

"And did the Baron favor the customs of L'Ollonais?" Harry asked.

She shook her head. "Spanish merchants would fight till the end because they knew

L'Ollonais would grant them no mercy. They had no cause to surrender when doing so meant they risked a woolding or some such torment. The Baron would, however, unleash his anger upon those that tested his patience, especially those who did not surrender soon enough. I saw him cut the tongue from a Spanish captain who dared curse him. He despised the Spanish as much as L'Ollonais had because when they were shipwrecked near Campeche, Spanish soldiers attacked them and killed nearly everyone. L'Ollonais and my father survived by covering themselves in blood and hiding amongst the dead."

"I heard tell you did not opt to cut tongue or heart from a man—you cut his cock."

She remembered the moment. A man by the name of Benjamin Matthews, formerly of the British Navy, had turned to the more lucrative options afforded by the slave trade. Matthews had boasted that if she tried to raid one of his ships, he would give chase, emerge the victor, and make her suck the cock of every member of his crew. She little cared what others said, being accustomed to the many threats men levied her way, the promised punishments made more savage for her crime of being a woman or a negress. But she did take satisfaction when she proved the victor over one of his slave ships—captained by Matthews himself. She had had him tied to the mizzenmast.

"'Tis certain I'll be taking your cock," she had smirked to him before yanking open his fall, making the buttons scatter over the deck. She had then asked for a hanger with a dull blade. His bloodcurdling cries as the hanger hacked at his member had been unlike any sound she had ever heard before. Several members of Matthews' crew bearing witness had retched, sobbed, or pissed their breeches.

"A pirate's greatest weapon is fear," she explained to Harry. "My father told me to make my mark if I wanted to captain the *Bloody Baron*. I had to prove myself as bold as any man—nay, bolder."

"And I thought you had cock cut off for mere sport."

He stroked himself, and she noticed a hardness returning to his member. She tried to ignore it, as well as the perk of interest in her own body and curiosity as to whether or not he could sustain an erection after all this time. The whores she had overheard always rejoiced in the fact that men could not last beyond one fucking.

"Care for another go?" Harry asked as he pulled his pole to stiffness.

Inadvertently, she licked her bottom lip. His arse tightened as his hips lifted. But she had strapped her weapons back in place upon her body. She had no plans to tarry. At times, after congress, she would allow herself to lay entwined in the limbs of a doxy. The softness of their bodies reminded her of how she felt being held by her mother before malaria claimed the one person she had ever trusted, ever loved.

But it was safer to spend the night on her ship, especially if Vane wanted her hurt or dead.

"If you breathe a word of what happened, you'll make Poirier a happier man," she warned with narrowed eyes, sickened by the thought of him boasting of his conquest to her crew. Would her men see her more as a woman and less a captain?

"You think I've a need to boast?" he returned.

"You're a man, are you not?"

"But I'm not stupid."

Satisfied for the present, she pulled open the door.

"Nevertheless," he said, "I be at your disposal, Captain, when next you require my services."

Not bloody likely, she thought to herself, walking out the door without acknowledging what he had said and leaving him to find his own needle and thread to patch his breeches.

Already she felt as if she had made a grave mistake in laying with Harry, a mistake that she would come to regret with every fiber of her being.

CHAPTER SEVEN

~ 1714, Seas off New Providence ~

Though Poirier had said nothing when La Croix announced Harry as the new first mate, his anger had been evident in the way the pupils of his grey eyes constricted and his thin lips thinned even further. She expected that after suffering such an insult, he would quit the *Bloody Baron,* but Poirier remained and grudgingly suffered Harry's sudden elevation from slave to first mate.

But because she still regretted her decision to lay with Harry, she often ordered him about as if he were still her slave, making him undertake menial tasks such as cleaning out the livestock pens or manning the crow's nest. She had expected him to remind her that he was now her first mate, but he made no complaints. The grin in his eyes—as if he understood the motives behind her commands—irked her more than any objection. After setting sail from Nassau, Harry did not renew his offer, but she would catch him eying her with an intense hunger that spoke to her own. She wanted to return to port and fuck a dozen whores to purge Harry from her system, but her men would grow restless on land, and a number of them had squandered their spoils already.

"I think we know her," said Harry as he stood to larboard beside La Croix .

La Croix eyed the ship through the telescope, and her nerves rose to attention. She recognized the sloop, though she bore a new name, *La Déesse.* It was Delacroix.

"He's spotted us," La Croix observed of the sails unfurling upon the other ship. She handed the telescope to Harry, who confirmed her findings.

"You think you can catch her?" he asked.

She smiled, knowing what the *Bloody Baron* was capable of. "Delacroix might have the lighter sloop, but she cannot fly as well as the *Baron.*"

She turned to the crewmembers, who, sensing something afoot, had gathered behind her, and rallied them, "'Tis Delacroix, the coward! Recall how he left us to fend for ourselves against an East Indiaman and a British third rate! He cared only to save himself! Remember your fallen brethren and avenge their deaths!"

The crew roared.

"Fly every stitch of canvas!" she cried. "The coward will not be getting away from us."

La Croix climbed the rigging, relishing the wind howling past her as the *Baron* cut through the water in full sail.

In less than half an hour, the *Baron* was close to firing distance. A canon from the *La Déesse* threw water into the air dozens of yards in front of the *Baron*.

"He be afraid," observed Harry after informing her the cannons were ready and the men armed.

"He was always a bit eager," La Croix said, returning to the deck. "Let him fire away. We'll hold steady till we're within range."

As the *Baron* neared the *La Déesse,* La Croix could feel anticipation tingling in every nerve. The sloops exchanged fire, but her crew, being the more disciplined of the two, found their mark more often, blasting the rudder off the *La Déesse* and taking away her steering.

"She's ours now," Poirer said to La Croix.

She would rather take her prize undamaged, but it was more important to capture Delacroix.

"Grenades and firearms first," she ordered, "then prepare to board."

The *Baron* pulled up to starboard of the *La Déesse.* A portion of La Croix's crew threw grenades and fired off their muskets while other crewmembers prepared the boarding planks, but the crew of the *La Déesse* were also prepared, returning fire. A grenade splintered the wood beside La Croix.

"I'll take him for you," Harry told La Croix.

She glared at him. "Do you think me a coward?"

"Delacroix and his crew know they be dead men if you capture them. They'll stop at nothing."

"I can't expect my men to commit themselves more than I do myself."

A canon shot from the *La Déesse* took out two of the cannons below, the blast throwing La Croix and Harry to the deck.

"*Putain*," La Croix cursed before scrambling back to her feet.

The crew of the *La Déesse* had managed to

dislodge all but one of the boarding planks and was about to shove away the last when Harry tossed a grenade into their midst and charged onto the plank before the *La Déesse* crew could recover. La Croix, her cutlass in one hand and her pistol in the other, followed. Though she recognized the men of the *La Déesse*, had even favored a number of them when they crewed the *Baron*, she had to blind herself to their faces. When she sliced them with her cutlass, they were the enemy, no different than the British who would see her hung at Gallow's Point. Only when she came face to face with Noah, a runaway slave not eight and ten, did she hesitate. The young man had been more than grateful when she had taken him aboard the *Baron* three years ago. She saw the remorse in his large brown eyes, saw his whole body shaking when he raised his sword to her.

"Was I not a *mère* to you?" she asked him over the sounds of gunfire, clashing blades, and men grunting and groaning. "If your owner had caught up to you, you would have died rotting in a crow's cage. I gave you life, the chance to become a man."

He looked ready to cry. He lowered his sword.

"You gave me new life. It is yours, then, to take away."

She looked him over. Noah would not have wanted to betray her, but, likely, he could not have defied Delacroix without risking his life at the time. Still, he ought to have chosen death. She admired him for choosing it now.

One of her crew, Sampson, stumbled up to her. "Captain! Their canons opened a seam aboard the *Baron.*"

"Surely Francois can patch it with oakum and powder," she answered, her gaze upon Noah, who did not take the opportunity to escape.

"Francois would have a word with you on it."

"Have him talk to Harry."

"I can't find Harry."

"I saw Harry," Noah offered. "He went into the captain's quarters."

La Croix motioned to Sampson and called out to Jacq, who had just thrust a bayonet into another man, to follow her.

"Can I come with?" Noah asked.

Assessing the sincerity in his eyes, she replied, "I may kill you yet, *mon enfant.*"

"Aye, Captain."

"Very well, then."

They made their way to Delacroix's cabin.

"I was about to look for you, Capitaine," said Delacroix, standing in the middle of the cabin in a scarlet coat that likely once belonged to an officer of the British army. Behind him, a large bearded man with arms thick as tree trunks, held a pistol to Harry's head. Rope bound Harry's arms to his sides.

Aside from a bruise at his temple and blood darkening his arm, Harry appeared to have sustained no significant injury.

"Order your men back aboard the *Baron*," Delacroix said, "lest you wish to see your precious first mate's brains spilled upon my floor."

"Captain La Croix would happily trade my death for yours," Harry sneered.

La Croix narrowed her eyes at Delacroix. "You think I would parley with a coward?"

Delacroix pressed his lips into a thin line. "You've no choice, Capitaine."

The boom of cannonfire, followed by a loud crack, much creaking, and the splash of a large object striking water drew their attention. Sampson ran to the window.

"They've shot the top of our mizzenmast!" he cried.

"We could bludgeon each other all day," Delacroix said, "but that would do neither of us any good."

He grabbed a knife from his table and shoved into Harry's rib. After withdrawing the knife, he turned back to La Croix. "Make your decision soon, Capitaine."

"Kill him!" Harry grimaced, his eyes bulging.

La Croix looked at the crimson quickly staining through Harry's clothes. She turned to Sampson. "Order the men to fall back."

"No!"

Ignoring Harry, she turned to Delacroix. "Even if you survive this day, your death will come soon enough."

"It matters not," Delacroix replied. "Yours is as likely to come before mine. Only a woman won't be spared as much as a man. I wonder that your father did not take that into account when he gave the *Baron* to you."

"Bloody hell, kill him!" Harry grunted.

"This is my score to settle, not yours," she replied as she glared at Delacroix.

"You may have your first mate back when we are clear to sail," said Delacroix.

"Tell your men to stand down," she said through gritted teeth.

After emerging from the cabin together, the bearded man dragging Harry behind them, Delacroix ordered the cease-fire from his crew.

"Shall we collect our wounded?" Jacq asked her.

She looked at Harry and replied, "Quickly."

When Noah moved to follow Jacq, Delacroix stopped him. "You're not thinking to rejoin the *Bloody Baron*?"

"What do you want with a boy?" La Croix demanded.

"Noah stays. And you had best board your ship, Capitaine. There be only so much blood Harry can lose."

"Give me Harry first."

"No, no. I keep Harry till we're ready to sail. Then I'll send him over in a rowboat."

"If you think to foil me, I'll cut out your bollocks and make you swallow them—before I dig out your eyes."

With a final glare, La Croix followed her men

back across the planks. They disengaged planks, hooks and ropes from the *La Déesse*. As Delacroix's crew prepared to sail away, La Croix felt as if she might explode with rage. She had given orders for her crew to ready the cannons to sink the *La Déesse* if Delacroix did not follow through. The *La Déesse* began to pull away. Her gaze did not leave the deck where the bearded man still held a pistol to Harry.

"Return the Englishman to them," Delacroix ordered.

Without removing Harry's bonds, the bearded man picked Harry up and tossed him into the sea. La Croix nearly threw off her coat and dove in after. But Noah had jumped in first. Harry did his best to tread water, but weakened from the loss of blood, he started to sink. Knife in hand, Noah cut away his bonds. Meanwhile, Sampson had strapped a rope about his waist and dove in. He grabbed Harry, and the crew pulled them both aboard the *Baron*. A rope was thrown to Noah, who climbed aboard shortly after.

Once the threesome were safe on deck, La Croix glanced up to see the *La Déesse* quickly moving out of firing range. She thought about giving chase, but with their mizzenmast broken, they were not likely to catch Delacroix.

"Why—didn't—you—kill him?" Harry gasped from where he lay.

"Take the fool to Mr. Adams," she ordered Sampson before turning around kicking a barrel of muskets. She was furious that Delacroix had gotten away unscathed. But she was more furious at the possible answer to Harry's question.

After she vented her wrath by kicking and knocking over the inanimate objects before her, she went below deck to where Mr. Adams, the surgeon and only other Englishman she allowed aboard the ship, was stitching Harry's wound.

"I'm—sorry—Captain," Harry gasped upon seeing her.

"He'll mend," Mr. Adams told her. "The knife missed vital organs."

She grunted and left. For a fortnight after, she refused to speak a word to Harry.

CHAPTER EIGHT

Having refitted the *Baron* after their confrontation with Delacroix, La Croix treated the men to a night of rum and whoring. The men were glad to be back in Nassau. Sitting in a tavern, La Croix pretended not to notice the number of whores that approached Harry at the bar. His fine countenance, often clean-shaven or graced with a faint stubble that lent him a proper rough and masculine quality without appearing the customary uncouth and dirty pirate, distracted from the fact that he had lost his right hand. His wound had healed well, and he was near to his former form.

Hoping to quell her jealousy by altering the position of her body, La Croix leaned away from the table onto the hindlegs of her chair while her quartermaster drank down his rum and laughed at some quip Poirer had made about Stede Bonnet. A flaxen haired beauty at Harry's left fluttered her lashes from behind her fan while a brunette vied for his attentions from his right side. Both harlots were English, like Harry, and conversed easily with him.

"Will you not partake, Capitaine?" Francois, her quartermaster asked as he scooped the barmaid holding his jug of rum onto his lap.

"*Non*," La Croix answered. Harry would have known not to even ask. As a woman and a negress, she could not let down her guard nor spare the slightest show of weakness.

And she preferred to find revelry not in rum or brandy but in fucking.

Ever since she had lain with Harry that one night, she had sought to recreate the heights he had taken her body. She fucked whores light and dark, slender and plump. She fucked them one, two, or three at a time. But none compared to Harry. The whores could not pound her as brutally as Harry could, and La Croix liked it rough. Recalling that night and how she had ridden his cock made her want to throw herself across the tavern and impale herself upon him.

But it was enough that she had lain with him once and made him her first mate. If she granted him too much, his esteem of himself would surely inflate. If only he were still her slave; then, there would be much she could make him do...

The blonde beside Harry gave a high-pitched giggle, sounding no older than a child in leading strings. La Croix realized she was looking at him again when she found herself caught in the icy blue crystals of his irises. He had turned around, leaning back on his left arm against the bar, the two harlots still engaged in tempting him, but he paid them little heed. La Croix considered shifting her gaze and feigning indifference, but she was momentarily caught. From his penetrating stare of her, there was no mistaking whom he wanted to fuck tonight.

Her cunnie pulsed.

Tearing herself from his gaze, she looked about the tavern and saw Rosalina, whom she had bedded before. The Spanish Creole gave her a wide smile. With a nod, La Croix motioned for the Creole to approach. Hips swaying, Rosalina made her way to La Croix. The ebony-haired harlot left behind three sailors who would have been more than eager to have her attentions for the night. If she did not favor the company of La Croix, she certainly favored La Croix's more generous coin-purse.

Rosalina sat herself on La Croix's lap. La Croix eyed Rosalina's many layers of clothing and the corset that forced the body into a conical shape. She knew not that she had the patience to undress Rosalina tonight.

"I worried that you might not return," Rosalina purred. "I had heard that merchants in Florida had commissioned two sloops to hunt down pirates."

"They would be after bigger fish," La Croix replied, eying the swollen orbs that Rosalina presented before her face. "Vane or Teach."

"But you've had many a successful raid and plunder."

"I have."

"Then you should boast of them."

"What purpose would that serve, *ma cheri*?"

Rosalina's eyes glimmered with emotion, and for a moment La Croix thought the harlot to be falling in love. Rosalina traced La Croix's bottom lip with her slender finger. "A man would take every chance to boast, though his accomplishments were not half yours."

Rosalina placed her mouth next to La Croix's ear and spoke in husky tones. "And you fuck better, too."

La Croix grinned. Grasping the woman by the chin, La Croix shoved their mouths together. She kissed Rosalina full on the lips, till Rosalina parted hers, inviting the invasion of La Croix's tongue. She tasted of molasses to La Croix, who plumbed the depths of her mouth to the stares of many about the tavern.

Rosalina cupped La Croix's jaw in both hands, murmuring against her lips, "Come, let me worship you tonight, La Capitana."

She grabbed La Croix by the hand and pulled her up as she gave La Croix her most seductive smile. La Croix allowed Rosalina to lead her up the stairs, noticing that Harry's gaze followed her.

As soon as Rosalina closed the door to a room behind them, the two women fell into another passionate kiss, lips crushed to lips. Unable to quench her true thirst, La Croix sucked upon Rosalina's mouth with uncommon fervor. Though Rosalina was no weakling, she could not kiss with the same strength as a man, and though La Croix had not thought she would care how she was kissed, she had enjoyed the brute force Harry had imposed in his kisses.

Their lips still locked, Rosalina began to unbutton La Croix's waistcoat. She yanked off La Croix's coat, followed by the waistcoat. With impatience, she pulled down La Croix's braces and, yanking the shirt from the breeches, thrust her hands up to palm the breasts, which La Croix, anticipating a night of debauchery, had not bound. Holding Rosalina by the back of her head, La Croix thrust her tongue into Rosalina's warm, wet mouth. Rosalina squeezed La Croix's breasts and rolled the nipples between her fingers. Her hand traveled down to La Croix's crotch.

"Undress first," La Croix ordered. She did not care for the voluminous garments that women had to adorn. After donning breeches for the first time, she had vowed never to wear a gown or petticoats again.

She also wanted to ensure that Rosalina hid no weapon, like the strumpet from the brothel earlier in the year. Standing a safe distance, she watched as Rosalina removed the pins in her gown.

"I overheard Poirier grouse about your first

mate," Rosalina remarked as she slid the bodice of her gown down her shoulders. "I would be weary of Poirier."

La Croix grunted in acknowledgment. Though Poirier had served on the *Bloody Baron* since the days of her father, who had bid the man to look after his daughter, La Croix understood that resentment could change a man.

"I never would have thought you to select an Englishman as your first mate," Rosalina continued, "though he is a fine specimen of man."

La Croix stared at Rosalina. What did the wench imply?

La Croix smirked. "You think I chose him for his beauty?"

"Not at all, La Capitana. I can see how your men respect, or perhaps fear, him, but I am uneasy to have a man such as him fill such a role of importance."

La Croix crossed her arms. She did not pay the whore for dialogue, but Rosalina was smarter than most strumpets. She also had the ears of a bat, and she often shared what she had heard with La Croix. It was Rosalina who had learned that Vane had left one of his boats unattended at the docks, a situation that La Croix had taken advantage of. So La Croix tolerated Rosalina more than she would others of her sex.

"And why be that, *ma cherí*?"

"I should not wish you to come to harm, La Capitana."

Rosalina had divested her skirt and petticoats. Convinced that Rosalina hid no weapons, La Croix strode over to unlace the Creole's corset.

"Harry had the chance to kill me but didn't," La Croix supplied, though she knew that did not mean Harry would refrain from doing so if another opportunity presented itself.

"He could break your heart."

La Croix paused, then threw back her head and laughed. "You jest. I would sooner be tarred and feathered than fall prey to such foolishness."

"But I saw the manner in which you looked at him."

La Croix continued unlacing the corset. "That look was one of lust, not love."

"Love can bloom from lust."

"I am incapable of love."

"With respect, La Capitana, you are capable of it if your mother loved you as much as you have told me."

"But to love a *man*? You know as well as I the treachery their sex is capable of." She thought of the man who had owned and raped her mother. She did not doubt that the Baron, for all his affection for her mother, had also been guilty of rape and that she was a child of such an act. La Croix continued, "I could live a hundred years, and my deeds could not match the evil their kind can amass in a sennight. They are disgusting creatures."

She spat on the floor for emphasis.

"And yet we are not immune to them. Especially one such as Harry. He is dangerous, and perhaps because of that, he is exciting. He means to have you, and I think he'll not stop till he does."

La Croix turned Rosalina around and pulled the corset off. Rosalina removed her chemise and stood in only her stockings and garters.

"He lusts for me," La Croix admitted, "but he is not the only one among my crew."

"But he is the only one you have allowed between your legs."

La Croix stared at Rosalina, wondering how the wench knew. Had Harry boasted of it? She would drive a dagger into his chest if he had.

As if reading her thoughts, Rosalina added, "I guessed as much. I saw the way he looks at you, and you at him."

La Croix scoffed. Again with the looks. Ready to be done with conversing, La Croix groped a breast.

Rosalina purred but continued to talk. "He is a determined sort of fellow, is he not?"

La Croix chose not to answer, agreeing only in silence. Instead, she lowered her head and drew one of Rosalina's plump nipples in her mouth. She sucked on it gently at first, teasing it to harden further, fuller between her lips. Hearing Rosalina moan, La Croix sucked harder until Rosalina gasped in a mixture of pleasure and pain.

"And he has you in his sights, La Capitana," Rosalina said, offering her other breast and nipple to La Croix.

"He has whores enough to busy himself with," La Croix replied.

"But whores can be gotten for two a half-piece. In our seas, there be none like you."

Though she would have liked to consider herself superior to others of her sex, she said, "But to a man, cunnie be cunnie. If it be tight about his cock, he'll not mind who he be laying with."

Rosalina shook her head. "He eyes you with a hunger unlike any I have seen in a man."

"Are you jealous?"

Rosalina stared at La Croix, affection shining from her eyes. "As I said, La Capitana, I have no wish to see you harmed, in any manner."

"Worry not. I mean to give him no encouragement, and he will find another to fix upon in due course. Perhaps he will attempt to seduce the daughter of a wealthy plantation owner."

To indicate she was done with th discourse, La Croix crushed her lips atop Rosalina's. They stumbled toward the bed and collapsed atop it. La Croix rolled Rosalina under her and pinned her hands above her head. Rosalina's eyes widened, unaccustomed to the rough handling. A rare verve coursed through La Croix's veins. She felt the need to impose her command. She slid her hand between Rosalina's thighs and found the wench wet with arousal. As she rubbed, Rosalina writhed in pleasure. After several minutes, Rosalina cried out in completion. La Croix withdrew her hand

and brushed it over the wench's cheek, leaving traces of Rosalina's own dew upon her face. She then pushed her fingers into Rosalina's mouth. Rosalina tongued La Croix's fingers, lapping at her own juices.

"I must pleasure you now, La Capitana," Rosalina said.

Exchanging positions, La Croix lay upon her back and allowed Rosalina to throw up her shirt and kiss and fondle her breasts. The wench spent too much time there, and La Croix had to push her head down to indicate she was ready for the main repast. Complying, Rosalina assisted La Croix from her boots and stockings. She then undid the buttons of the breeches before sliding them past La Croix's hips, laying bare her lower body. La Croix spread her legs, and Rosalina dove between them. La Croix sighed with satisfaction as Rosalina's tongue began to travel up and down her folds. Spreading her thighs further apart, La Croix angled her hips to give Rosalina better access. When Rosalina began to trace lines around her pleasure bud, a low moan escaped La Croix.

"Mmm," Rosalina purred. "How tantalizing you taste."

Ravenously, she lapped at La Croix's moist flesh. La Croix relaxed into the bed and tried not to compare Rosalina to Harry. Should she not prefer the softer, lighter touch of a woman? Rosalina knew her way about La Croix's cunnie, knew how to draw pleasure from her body, but the hollow inside her wanted penetration. Hard penetration.

Rosalina teased the rosebud from between the folds and sank two digits into La Croix's slit. La Croix wondered which of the whores Harry was likely bedding. Would it be the blonde with her square jaw and large bosom? Or the slim brunette who looked as if she barely had six and ten years to her name? How would he bed a whore? Would he take her roughly? Quickly? Would he seek only his pleasure, as most men did? Or would he arouse her to distraction, as he had done to her?

Jealousy flared in La Croix's bosom. She did not like the sentiment. She ground herself into Rosalina's mouth and hand, hoping her climax would wash away the ugly feeling. But it was not enough. She needed more force.

"Fetch a phallus."

Rosalina went to the sideboard and returned

with a wooden dildo. She nestled it between La Croix's folds and gently pushed it in.

"More," La Croix demanded.

Rosalina wedged the length of the phallus into La Croix, who closed her eyes to better savor the hardness between her legs. And yet a real cock felt better. Why was that?

Rosalina withdrew the dildo before pushing it back in.

"Harder," La Croix instructed. Propping herself up on her elbows, she watched as Rosalina pulled and pushed the false cock in and out of her cunnie. "Further."

She rubbed her clitoris as Rosalina worked the dildo. Visions of Harry drilling into her taunted her. She erupted to the memory of riding atop him, his hook pressing into her hip. As she lay back and soaked in the bliss of her climax, Rosalina's words returned to her:

He means to have you, and I think he'll not stop till he does.

CHAPTER NINE

Having dressed and left the room where Rosalina had elected to rest, still naked, upon the bed, La Croix told herself that the wench fretted for no reason. If Harry had truly wanted her as much as Rosalina claimed, he would have made advances. And if he did attempt to seduce her, she would make him rue his mistake. But how might she do so? Now that he was first mate, she could not have him flogged before the crew as she had done so in the past. He might lose his standing among some of the men.

Perhaps she could cut him, wounding him enough to fortify her message. Or kick him in the cods. Nay, she would twist and squeeze them first, then kick him. Warmed at the thought, La Croix continued down the hall toward the stairs. But as she passed one of the rooms, she heard a voice cry out, "Nay! You are far too large!"

Stepping over a crew member slumped upon the floor, sleeping away his intoxication, La Croix peered through the crack in the door and saw a shirtless man with his breeches down past his knees. Without thinking, she licked her bottom lip at the sight of the man's bare muscular buttocks.

Harry.

The brunette, wearing only her corset and shift, knelt before him, staring at his crotch.

"Come, a wench as pretty as you must have had larger," he dismissed with a stroke of his cock.

"I can fit him," declared the blond strumpet, still fully dressed, as she came up behind him.

"In due time, love," Harry told her. "I mean to attend you both."

Jealousy stirred once more within La Croix. She ought to continue on her way, but her legs would not move.

Harry turned to the brunette. "If you'll not have me in your cunnie, take me into your mouth."

The harlot took his member and began bobbing up and down the shaft. La Croix felt warmth stirring in her loins, craving a taste herself. The blonde wrapped her arms about Harry and caressed his chiseled body.

Not satisfied with the depth to which the brunette swallowed his cock, Harry pushed her head down, but she started to choke. La Croix smirked.

"Permit me," the blonde said and quickly went down to her knees.

Grabbing his cock, she swallowed a good length ravenously. La Croix wondered if she could take as many inches of Harry as the blonde did. She wanted to think she could do more, though she had little practice in swallowing cock. Intrigued, she watched as the cheeks of the blonde caved inward, noting how she cradled his bollocks.

Harry moaned in approval. "You must fancy cockmeat a great deal."

The whore drew her tongue along the underside of his shaft. "'Tis finer than beefsteak, Captain."

La Croix started at the word. How dare Harry tell those two whores that he was captain? He needed no such lie to impress them into his bed. She wondered if being captain was one of his aspirations.

"I not be captain," Harry replied to La Croix's satisfaction.

"You ought to be. You'd be much better than that meager. She must be half man for a true woman would not do as she does –"

Smack!

The blonde fell to the floor, tears blurring her eyes.

"You not be worth a strand of her hair," Harry said.

La Croix smiled, impressed by his loyalty.

"If I hear you speak another ill word of Captain La Croix, I'll do more than cuff the side of your head," Harry warned. "Now get back here and finish your feasting."

The blonde crawled back onto her knees and took his cock once more but without her former appetite. Harry did not seem to mind and thrust his hips at her face.

Fuck her till she chokes, La Croix silently ordered him.

He thrust harder, faster. She gagged, but he grabbed her by the hair and kept on pummeling.

The heat between La Croix's thighs

intensified. She wanted to touch of his cock.

"Gah, gah, gah," she croaked.

Make her cry, La Croix bid him.

But he withdrew. A length of spittle and mettle bridged the tip of his cock and her lips. He smeared the wetness over her mouth and chin.

"On the bed, both of you," he ordered. "On your hands and knees. I want to see your arses."

Without hesitating a second, they did as instructed, settling themselves side-by-side.

"Come closer," he said till they were at the edge of the bed. He flipped up the chemise of the brunette, revealing rounded buttocks. He did the same to the many layers of skirt and petticoats of the blonde. Her rump was pale and small. La Croix preferred a more supple derrière and wondered which one Harry preferred.

He aimed his length at the blonde and rubbed it between her legs. She moaned. By her gasp, La Croix assumed Harry had plunged himself into her hole. With his hand on her hip, he smacked his pelvis into her rear. She cried out with every thrust. La Croix remembered well how his cock had filled her own cunnie. She very much envied the strumpet, and her irritation grew, knowing that she would not get to savor the feel of him filling her.

After several minutes, Harry withdrew and stood behind the brunette. She began to quiver even before he touched her.

"Worry not," Harry assured as he rubbed her lower back.

Why did he not simply shove himself into her, La Croix wondered. The woman was a whore, not his lover.

"Indeed," said the blonde, "I've not felt anything finer."

"How be this?" he inquired, reaching down to the floor where his coat lay and fishing out a coin. "Heads, I enter you slow. Tails, I enter in one quick motion. If I were you, I should prefer the latter."

He flipped the coin into the air, caught it, and pressed it to his forearm. Lifting his hand, he announced, "Tails."

She groaned in dismay. He tossed the coin to her before settling himself behind her once more. Without ceremony, he plunged in. She emitted a long, high-pitched squeal. He allowed her a moment to adjust to the intrusion before slowly beginning to thrust. Her screams eventually grew shorter and softer.

"Ah, you feel quite fine," he said.

The screams of the brunette softened into groans. The blonde grew visibly impatient.

"Can it be my turn now?" she asked.

Obliging, Harry withdrew from the brunette and switched to fucking the blonde.

She cried out at the force with which he plunged into her, but soon she was groaning in pleasure. Jealousy flared within La Croix, causing her arousal to deepen.

The blonde gave a wail and shuddered as she spent. Harry thrusted into her vigorously, the force of sending her toward the headboard. He pulled out, and she collapsed onto the bed. The brunette looked on with envy.

Harry smacked the blonde's arse. "Get up and undress each other."

She got off the bed, and he took her place after kicking off his breeches. Sitting with his back against the headboard, his legs stretched before him, he stroked himself as the women proceeded to disrobe one another.

"Now kiss and fondle each other," he said

when they were both naked.

The blonde cupped the back of the brunette's head and drew her mouth to her own painted lips. The brunette groped the breasts of the blonde and rolled the orbs.

"Now suckle her teats," Harry instructed.

The brunette lowered her head and took a nipple into her mouth. La Croix's mouth watered. Though she did not favor the paleness of the blonde, she would fuck her if given the chance. She would try to match the force with which Harry had shoved into her. Her legs quivered as she wondered how it would feel to be fucked with such strength. She glanced at the rod protruding from his pelvis, and the ache between her legs throbbed.

The blonde slid her hand between the thighs of the brunette, stroking till the brunette purred and moaned. Crooking a finger, Harry beckoned for the brunette to come over. He pulled her over him and had her straddle his hips before pushing her down onto his cock. She gasped, then whimpered.

"And what am I to do?" the blonde asked.

"Whatever you wish," he answered.

She chose to straddle him in front of the brunette and crushed her mouth to his. She kissed him with passion while she rubbed her breasts against his chest. The sounds of the bed creaking, of flesh smacking against flesh, the grunting, groaning, and moaning became too much for La Croix.

Flushing with disquiet and yearning, she forced herself to walk away. As she made her way along the corridor and down the stairs, she considered having a tankard of rum. Surely a little could do no harm? And it might calm the agitation inside her.

But she could not allow herself the temptation. It did not please her that she rarely craved rum till now. Till Harry.

She walked out of the tavern and headed to the beach, where she inhaled the salty damp air and listened to the soft purr of the waves as they approached shore. The sun, heading for the horizon, cast the sky in vibrant hues of orange and rose. Picking up a small rock, La Croix hurled it as far as she could into the water.

She had erred. She ought to have kept Harry a slave. For a long spell, she had not permitted him to come ashore. She remembered the flicker of disappointment the first time she had denied his request, but he had subsequently masked any anger well, even when her crew taunted him with tales of the fine rum and bawdy whores that could be had in town.

But what was done was done. Her crew did well with Harry as first mate, and she had no wish to appear fickle. She simply had to find a way to eliminate her carnal desire of him.

But how?

With a frustrated grunt, she leaned against one of the thick branches of a sea grape. The sea grape was her favorite type of plant and did not grow in the manner of most trees. Instead of shooting towards the sky, it extended sideways, sometimes crawling along the ground, its branches thick as trunks.

Despite having wiped herself after her romp with Rosalina, new moisture now soaked the crotch of her breeches.

Damn Harry.

Catching the soft tread of boots upon sand, she whipped out her dagger and faced the form ambling toward her.

"Harry," she whispered before relaxing and sheathing her weapon.

"Captain," he greeted.

As if his presence bored her instead of sparking her nerves, she leaned back against the tree and gazed out at the sunset with a yawn.

Harry grinned. "Had a good go at Rosalina?"

Not nearly as well as you had with your two whores, she nearly replied. Aloud, she said, "She be a decent fuck."

"I think half your men would give their right arm to tumble her, but she always favors you."

"And why wouldn't she?"

His gaze upon her intensified. "Indeed. I know whom I'd favor as well."

Her heart skittered as she spared him a glance. Beneath his stare, she suddenly felt like a cut of steak he wanted to devour.

"You come here to tell me that?" she asked with some disgust.

"I come here to tell you that if you need a better tumble than what Rosalina can offer, you know where to find it."

She doubted she could swallow if her life depended upon it. Though he stood an arm's length away, he felt much closer.

She smirked. "You think you can be a better fuck than Rosalina?"

He continued to stare at her, unblinking with those haunting eyes of his. "I know it...and you do, too."

When he closed the distance between them, he took the air from her with the force of a gale. A part of her wanted to launch herself at him and take him upon the sand, showing the sun and waves the depths of their carnal passions.

Bracing his left arm against a branch above her, he leaned toward her. Her senses went to high alert—and anticipation. Did he mean to touch her? Kiss her?

Or neither.

A blast cracked the air and a searing pain exploded in her lower body.

CHAPTER TEN

Harry had betrayed her. And after she had saved his bloody life. How dare...

But he looked as stunned as she felt, his eyes wide with confusion. She realized the burning pain was concentrated in the back of her left thigh. The rustle of leaves drew their attention to the forestry where a man had turned his back to flee the scene. La Croix collapsed into her left side and grasped the back of her leg where blood coursed over her fingers.

"Captain!" Harry exclaimed, catching her.

"*Non!*" she cried. "Don't attend me—go after him!"

Harry hesitated a second, concern etched upon his brow as he gazed down upon her, before springing after the man, crashing into the flora like a wild boar bearing down on its meal. She did not doubt but that Harry, with his determination, would catch his quarry. She heard a thud, followed by the crush of leaves, that sent a few birds scattering to the skies. Pulling the kerchief that wrapped her locks, she tied it about her leg. Her flesh felt like it was being eaten by fire.

A minute later, Harry returned, dragging a young man behind him. The man had blood and bits of bark upon his forehead. Perhaps Harry had smacked him into a tree. Harry held the man's flintlock in his left hand. After dropping the man before La Croix, he drew out his sword and sank the blade into the man's leg. The man screamed.

As he kept the man pinned beneath his sword, Harry turned to La Croix. "I'll kill him swift. We ought get you to Mr. Adams."

La Croix glared at Harry, her patience thin as the pain in her leg threatened to spread. "Not before I ascertain who shot me."

Harry turned to the man and began twisting the sword in the man's leg. The latter howled in agony. "What be your name, lad?"

"J-James," the man sobbed. "P-Please don't kill me. I'll—I'll do as you please. Join your crew. Anything. Please."

La Croix examined the features of the man

and estimated he was barely twenty years of age. She did not recognize him and doubted they had crossed paths in any manner that would have caused him to hate her enough to want to kill her. Lest she or her crew had maimed or killed his father.

"Your full name," she demanded.

"J-James M-Mills."

The name was unfamiliar to her.

"Can I kill him now?" Harry asked.

"Please!"

Tears poured from the young man. The crotch of his pants darkened in color. Harry rolled his eyes as they caught the scent of urine. But La Croix held up her hand.

"Why did you take aim at me, James?" she asked. "Were you trying to kill me?"

He sobbed harder.

"Answer her," Harry growled.

The young man tried. "I—'Twas—Please... please don't kill me."

Exasperated, Harry drew out his sword only to plunge it into James' other leg. James gave another howl.

"Damnation, let him speak," La Croix yelled at

Harry over James' cries. She turned to the man, whose blood now coated the beach much more than her own. "Come, *mon enfant*, I will have mercy upon you if you tell me why you tried to kill me."

With his words mixed with the tears and mucus streaming, James blustered, "It was—it was M—Moll O'Leary. P—Promised me a piece if I—if I..."

"If you killed me?"

James nodded, his beautiful grey eyes full of tears.

"Where can I find this O'Leary?" she asked, her tone still gentle, almost motherly.

"In—the—the green thatched house off the main square."

"Did O'Leary tell you why he be wanting me dead?"

"N—no, ma'am."

"I don't believe him," Harry said.

La Croix did. She ordered Harry to load the flintlock.

James' eyes widened. "You—you promised me m—mercy."

"I did," she acknowledged, "and I'll keep my

118

word, *mon enfant*. You may choose your manner of death. 'Tis a luxury on most counts I would not grant to a man who tried to kill me. You may die by bullet or by hook."

Harry drew his hook across his throat to gesture what death by hook would entail. James fell into hysterical sobbing, pleading and begging.

"What be your choice, *mon enfant*?"

But James was crying too much to answer.

"By bullet then," La Croix said, "as it is far more merciful, and I did promise mercy."

While Harry finished loading the firearm with the bullet and powder, James tried to scramble away, but Harry knelt on the young man's chest.

"Open up," Harry ordered, pointing the barrel at James' mouth.

"Pleeeease..." James moaned.

"Trust me, you'll want the bullet," La Croix encouraged.

Quaking, James parted his lips. Harry shoved the flintlock into James' mouth. The man's teeth clattered about the barrel.

"'Tis a shame," Harry remarked. "He be a pretty lad."

Before La Croix could respond, Harry blew

James' brains onto the beach.

"O'Leary," La Croix muttered to herself, trying to think whom she knew with such a name. She grunted as the pain in her leg throbbed.

Harry scrambled to his feet. "I'll take care of this O'Leary. I think Mr. Adams be—"

"I want to see this O'Leary for myself," she told him. She handed him her dagger. "You'll get this bullet out from me."

Harry frowned but made no objections. He whipped off his coat and spread it upon the sand before taking her dagger. She lay down upon his coat and braced herself. She had been shot in the other leg before. At the time, however, her father had ordered her to drink three pints of rum before he had the surgeon remove the bullet.

At present, she had not the benefits of intoxication, but she wanted to find this O'Leary soon.

Harry ripped a larger hole into her breeches to access the wound. As the wound was high on her thigh, the back of his hand grazed the bottom of her arse. She grimaced as the dagger dug into her. He stopped to rip both sleeves of his shirt. He twisted one sleeve and offered it to her lips. She bit down on the fabric, grunting furiously when he dug the dagger back into her leg. Tears watered her eyes. It was a painful yet oddly intimate experience she shared with Harry. She could think of no other crew member, aside from Mr. Adams, whom she would allow this close to her body.

"Done!" Harry pronounced in triumph. With the bullet out, he wrapped the other shirtsleeve about her leg as a tourniquet.

She pushed herself up onto one leg, but the instant she put weight upon her wounded leg, she felt like crumbling.

"You'll make yourself bleed more, Captain," Harry said, holding her up.

She leaned against the tree, thinking she would have to find a horse to ride.

Harry shook the sand from his coat, put it on, and scooped her up.

"Here—" she objected.

"The main square be not far," he explained. "I'll carry you."

She did not much like the idea of being carried like a child in Harry's arms, but she wanted to find O'Leary badly enough that she allowed it.

By the time they came to the dwelling, it was dark. Harry had run most of the way, perhaps as eager as her to confront O'Leary. After setting her down, Harry pointed to the light glowing from behind drawn curtains. Someone was home. La Croix nodded. Harry knocked on the door.

"Who be there?" a woman asked.

"J-James," Harry replied, attempting to mimic the young man's higher tenor. "It be done."

There was a pause, followed by the click of the lock. The door opened a crack. Harry shoved his shoulder into the door, which nearly flew off its hinges as he barged in. A woman shrieked.

Not expecting Harry to stop short, La Croix bumped into him as she followed him inside.

"You," Harry said to the form that had fallen to the ground.

The woman tried to scurry away, but La Croix managed to shut the door and cover the door handle with her body.

"You," La Croix echoed as her gaze fell upon a woman with red locks and the initials "L" and "C" scarred into the sides of her face.

"Be you O'Leary?" Harry asked. He examined her cheeks. "You wear my handiwork well, love."

At that, she scrambled in a different direction, but Harry grabbed her by the hair and flung her into a chair. Standing behind her, he held his hook before her throat.

"I think our friend James was a'telling us that her name be Moll, mayhap Molly," Harry noted. He leaned toward her ear and spoke as soft as a lover. "Is that your name? Molly O'Leary?"

"What does it matter?" La Croix asked.

"Curious what name might grace her tombstone."

The whore's eyes did not widen in surprise for she already knew she was as good as dead.

Harry pressed the point of his hook into her throat. "Is it?"

"Aye," the whore squeaked.

"And who would pay for a tombstone for a whore?" La Croix asked.

Harry shrugged. "She may have family. A mother or father who might care what happened to their daughter."

He turned to the strumpet, who shivered in her seat, the color drained from her face. "Do you have a family, Molly?"

She nodded.

"Here in Nassau?"

"I-Ireland."

"They must miss their pretty lass."

La Croix winced as her leg throbbed in pain. Though Harry had carried her the distance from the beach, the journey had still put a strain on her leg. She considered telling Harry to kill the whore already, but she knew why he delayed.

A sob escaped Molly.

"Do they know what you've been up to here in Nassau?" Harry asked.

Looking down, she shook her head.

"We best inform them then. Wouldn't want them wonderin' what happened to dear little Molly. You know how to write, love?"

She didn't answer, but he asked for paper and pen. With her eyes still downcast, her bottom lip trembling, an occasional tremor running through her body, she pointed at the sideboard.

La Croix hobbled over and brought over the paper, quill and ink. She leaned against the table.

"A short letter will do," she informed Harry.

When Molly did not take up the quill, Harry shoved it into her hand and began to dictate. "Dearest Mother and Father. I write..."

He paused for her hand shook so violently she could barely sketch a letter. He cupped his hand about hers to assist her.

"I write to inform you of my death," he continued. "I have been a naughty whore here in Nassau and did try to kill the Baroness La Croix, a most feared and—"

He looked up at La Croix. "Do you prefer 'dreaded,' Captain?"

"Dreaded and terrible," La Croix supplied.

"Dreaded and terrible pirate captain. I must pay for my misdeeds. Please pray for my soul. Your loving lass, Molly."

She now sobbed as much as James had.

"Address it now," Harry directed.

La Croix looked at the barely legible letters, smothered with tears.

"We ought send them a memento to remember you by," Harry decided as he brushed his hook through her long reddish locks. He reached for his dagger and fit it into his hook. "Hold still, love."

Molly screamed. La Croix thought he meant to slash off a lock of her hair, but Harry had cut into her scalp. When he was done, the back of her head lay bald and bleeding. He dropped the scalp upon the table in front of her.

"You want I should shave her clean?" he asked La Croix, fingering what was left of Molly's hair above the ears.

"*Non*," she replied, fighting back the fatigue of her wound. "Let us determine how we mean to kill the wench. 'Tis a pity for her that I gave James all the mercy I can grant in a day."

"Indeed, you spared him far too easily. I only got to stab him twice with me sword."

Molly must have heard some of what they said for her sobbing grew louder.

"We gave James the option of death by bullet or hook," Harry said. "He received the former. Perhaps Molly here could have the latter. What think you, lass?"

The whore was in no condition to respond. La Croix leaned more upon the table. Her blood had soaked through the sleeve Harry had wrapped about her and reached all the way to her stockings.

"Captain?"

But La Croix felt her focus waning. She saw Harry press his lips in a grim line as he observed her. He drew out his sword and, with a sweep of his backhand, beheaded the strumpet. The severed head tumbled to the ground as the body fell forward onto the table, splattering blood onto La Croix. Harry caught her before she, too, slumped to the table. In her weakened state, she was vulnerable. A dishonest man could do much to take advantage of the situation.

However, she had no choice but to trust Harry.

CHAPTER ELEVEN

~ 1713, Bloody Baron ~

Pushing aside her vexation from her near rape aboard the merchant vessel, La Croix stared at Harry over the decanter she held. She recognized the look upon his face. It matched her own primal urges, but it would be folly to surrender to baser desires. She would have to relieve her agitation herself or wait until the *Bloody Baron* could pull into port and a suitable brothel could be found.

"You should apply a poultice for your wound," Harry said, standing an arm's length from where she sat in her large wing chair with scrolled arms and silk upholstery.

"Don't speak to me as if I were a child," she grumbled, irked that she craved him as much as she did. The scent of him, his potency mixed with sweat, blood, and gunpowder, filled her nostrils and tempted her senses. In the quiet of her cabin, it felt as if she and Harry were a world away from the rest of the crew, though she could hear them, faintly, singing and making merry with the barrels of wine from their bounty.

To fill the tense silence between them, she kicked aside the footstool and ordered, "Take off m' boots."

He knelt before her so that she could push one leg against his chest for leverage as he pulled the boot off her other leg. After removing the second boot, he dared caress the length of her calf through the silk stocking. She shivered at his touch. She ought to punish him for taking such a liberty. Instead, she took a swig from the decanter. Were she feeling more generous, she would have offered the wine to him. He knew better than to ask for any.

He stared at the leg he held and spoke in a low, gruff voice. "May I pleasure you, Captain?"

It was what she desired above all else. Her pulse quickened at the prospect. The area between her thighs warmed. Arousal throbbed in her loins.

Non. That was the proper response. The bloody *saluad.* How dare he put her in such a quandry? Men. Forever wanting a fuck. They would stop at naught in pursuit of cunnie. Anger flared, providing temporary relief from her lust.

Pulling her leg from him, she kicked him in the face. She briefly winced at the tug of discomfort, her action stretching the scar in the back of her leg. Her heartbeat quickened as she awaited his reaction. His countenance was turned away from her, and his lowered eyelids covered any anger that he might have felt. Her gaze dropped to his hook. It would take but seconds for him to wound her with it, or even kill her. That damn hook. She ought to make him take it off. With her crew merrymaking below deck, there might not be anyone to hear her cries.

He met her gaze, and she tensed, ready to bolt as far away from him as possible. She was a jellyfish taunting the larger, stronger shark.

"You disregarded my orders," she said. "I told you to desist."

A muscle rippled along his jaw. ""Your pardon, Captain. It won't happen again."

Emotion bolted up her spine. Her fear had not diminished, but arousal coursed even hotter through her.

"Still wish to pleasure me?" she sneered,

trying to contain her tremors.

"More than ever, Captain."

His gaze pierced her to the core, his answer liquefying her insides. She could make him service her, lick her cunt until she drenched his face with her ecstasy, while leaving his hardened arousal unattended. But she wondered that she had the patience to last without his cock.

Damn him. She would make him pay for this. Make him wish that she had never elevated him above his former status as a slave.

With her mood suddenly improved, she rose to her feet with a slowness that belied her eagerness. She stood close enough that she could feel his breath, heavy with desire. His nostrils flared at her nearness. She could bring her knee to his cods, as she had done many times before, though it was not as easy or as imposing as she would have liked for he stood much taller than she. Nay, she had more in store for him.

"You must earn such a privilege," she said.

As if sensing her thoughts, his lashes, soft and brown, fluttered, but he did not flinch.

"Strip," she commanded, "to the buff."

He removed his weapons first: his cutlass,

dagger and pistol. His gaze never left hers as he peeled off his coat. The intensity in his eyes made her wonder if she was not punishing herself as well by not tearing off his clothes herself, but she told herself that her forbearance would be rewarded. After dropping his coat, he undid the buttons of his waistcoat with uncharacteristic slowness. Was it his intention to stall his punishment, or did he mean to make her pay along with him?

While he shed his waistcoat and kicked off his boots, she went through the sideboard to find a slender strand of rope, several metal rings and her flogger. When she had all the items she wanted, she turned around to find Harry in glorious nakedness. Her gaze drank in his broad shoulders, chiseled torso, tapered hips, muscular legs, and, of course, that beautiful shaft protruding from between his thighs. She licked her bottom lip and felt her breeches grow damp.

Her gaze shifted from his erection to his hook. Her pulse quickened. Given what she contemplated, perhaps it would be wise to take all precautions.

"And your hook," she told him.

He raised a brow but did as she bid without objection. She shivered for he looked as ominous after removing the hook as he did retaining it. He set it gently aside.

She tossed him a yard of rope. "Tie your wrist to the top of my bedpost."

He bound himself to the post, facing away from the bed. After testing his bonds, she stepped onto the bed behind him and secured his other wrist to the opposite bedpost. She went back to stand before him to admire her bed's new ornament. She ran her fingers along the length of his arms. With his limbs stretched taut, the muscles in his arms bulged, inviting her to sink her teeth into their hard suppleness. She caressed his pectorals with fingers and lips, licking a stiff nipple before taking it into her mouth and sucking. She nibbled on the rosy flesh before drawing it into her mouth and sucking. Hard. He emitted a satisfied groan as his cock glanced upward. She transferred her attention to the other nipple, lapping hungrily before clamping down on the helpless bud with her teeth. Harry grunted. His body tightened. She continued her assault, alternating between teasing nibbles and painful bites. He clenched his jaw when she drew blood.

Retreating, she dared to look into his eyes. There was fire there but not anger. Yet.

She retrieved the flogger and caressed the leather tail before him. "I never allowed you could touch me. How many lashes do you think you merit for such insubordination?"

"Ten," he answered.

She was impressed that he did not attempt to eschew his punishment. Ten lashes was a sound number as he knew she would not go lightly with the falls. Nevertheless, she said, "Twenty be better. Plus, ten more for good measure, should you think to offer too low a number next time."

Unfurling the flogger, she struck him in the ribs, then the chest, and the thigh, deliberately allowing the tails to wrap about him for a harsher sting. He withstood the blows with barely a grunt until she caught him between the legs. He howled then. She allowed the pain to sink in before aiming for his cods. His body caved inward, and his left hand balled into a fist. Giving him a reprieve, she attacked his chest, striking at the nipple with her backhand. His body jerked when the leather bit into the sensitive nub.

Hearing the slap of leather against flesh, his muffled roars, seeing the crimson trail where the flogger had landed, made the blood pound within her. Her cunnie throbbed. She saw the glisten of moisture at the tip of his cock and decided that she would allow herself a taste. His shaft had lost none of its previous hardness, though she had expected it would wither beneath his beating. Kneeling before him, she gripped his length and licked away the drops of his desire. She fit her mouth over the flare of his member, felt his hardness calling to the ache between her legs. She slid her hand to his sack and cradled the orbs inside. She rolled and tugged them before giving them a vicious squeeze as her mouth sank down his shaft. She could not tell if his groan was one of pleasure or pain, or both.

She rose to resume the flogging. Her body yearned for his, and she unleashed her frustration by hitting him as hard as she could upon the arms, the chest, the sides of his arse, and his cock and cods. On the thirty-second blow, he was breathing heavily. Small beads of perspiration dotted his brow. And in his eyes, there was anger. She wondered what thoughts went through his head.

She guessed he wanted to do more than fuck her. With that assumption, she lashed at his groin with even greater vigor. His body trembled. To her surprise, his cock remained hard. She wrapped the flogger about his neck and pulled his head down toward her.

"That be more than thirty lashes," he grunted.

"Not by my count," she smirked. She thrilled to the mixture of anger and admiration in his countenance. "Indeed, there be naught to stop me from flogging you more. I could shred the flesh in front of you, give you scars to match the ones on your backside."

"If you would let me fuck you, I would bear as many lashes as you would give."

His words made her quiver. Did he mean what he said? Should she find out? She smiled, pretending to be amused. "I not be done."

Leaving the flogger about his neck, she stepped back and admired the virile animal at her mercy. Her gaze drank in the hard, taut muscles of his arms, his chest, and his legs. Like a wolf before raw kill, she salivated—but between the legs.

Retreating to the sideboard, she found another cord of rope and a pair of metal clamps joined by a chain. She affixed the clamps to his nipples. He gave a low groan, which grew into an agonized howl when she pulled on the chain. Grabbing his chin, she parted his lips, fit the chain between his teeth, and closed his mouth. His body quivered at the constant tugging on his nipples. Next, she tied the rope about his shaft and scrotum. She stepped back and slapped his cock, marveling at how hard it had remained throughout his torment. He grunted. She smacked his erection harder, then grabbed his bollocks and squeezed as hard as she could. With a roar, he convulsed against the pain, and she thought he might break the bedposts in twain. Heat surged through her. She yanked off the clamps to elicit another roar.

"Fuck me now, would you, knave?" she asked.

A light sheen of sweat glistened about his brow. She found his gaze upon her menacing, though she could not tell if she feared his anger or his lust more.

"Till kingdom come, Captain."

CHAPTER TWELVE

It took her several seconds to find her breath.

"And what makes you think you be worthy of my cunnie?" she inquired.

"You gave it once to me before."

"In a moment of weakness."

"If I recall, your cunnie liked my cock and was fair wet for me. I wager your cunnie be sodden with hunger now."

She frowned, not wanting to acknowledge what he said was true, but she admitted, "I do find flogging an Englishman to be quite pleasurable."

"Then let me pleasure you more, Captain." He jerked against his bonds. "Let me ravish your cunnie till you can scream no more."

"You pay whores in port for the use of their cunnies. What would you offer me?"

"Your cunnie be priceless."

She threw back her head and laughed.

"What do you want of me?" he asked.

He could have said he had given much to her already, more than any man had ever given of himself. Instead, he seemed ready to do more. As she considered her answer, she pulled her chair in front of him and, shedding her coat, lay it over the back of the chair.

"Do you wish to whip me more?" he offered.

She remembered he had pieces of eight, a supposed treasure he had kept hidden, but she had no desire to lower herself to the status of whore, even if she made him pay a grand sum for the privilege of her cunnie.

She unbuttoned her waistcoat, then grinned mischievously. "Would you take a dildo in your arse for me?"

At that he frowned. She was not surprised that he would rather take a lashing than be buggered. She slipped out of her waistcoat and pulled down her braces.

"Is that what my captain wishes?" he asked.

She returned a broad smile as she pulled the hem of her shirt from her breeches.

"If I can return the favor, then let's have at it."

She stared at him with wide eyes, surprised

that he would acquiesce to buggery but also at his proposal to bugger her.

He raised a brow. "Never been fucked in the arse before?"

She sucked in her breath, unsure if she ought to be aroused or repulsed.

He smiled. "It be a wondrous thing, Captain."

"For you perhaps."

At her expression of doubt, he said, "You may find you like my cock in your arse more than you like it in your cunnie."

"You buggered before?"

"Aye."

"Whores?"

"Aye."

"And you wish to treat me as one?"

He drew back. "Never, Captain."

She unbuttoned her breeches and let them fall to her feet. After stepping out of them, she slid off her stockings. Wearing only her shirt, she sat down in the chair and flung a leg over an armrest. "How can I be certain?"

"Certain of what, Captain?"

"Certain that you won't think me one of your sluts if I grant you a piece of my cunnie."

"You think I would allow a whore to do half what you have done to me?"

Her eyes steeled. "Indeed. *You* would sooner be *my* whore than I *yours*."

"Aye, use me, Captain. My cock be at your disposal."

She looked at the hard, pulsing length of meat. Finer than the sweetest papaya or the most succulent conch. She reached a hand beneath her shirt to touch herself. His gaze went straight to the area between her legs. He strained toward her, ravenous, like a shark scenting blood in the water.

Leaning her head back, she closed her eyes as she caressed her wet folds and toyed with the bud nestled between. He waited patiently as she brought herself closer and closer to the edge. Arousal, which had spread throughout her, began to condense to where the tips of her fingers met her flesh. She groped a breast through her shirt and bindings with the other hand. Pleasure boiled over, and she trembled as she spent.

When she opened her eyes, she was met with the intensity of Harry's bright blue eyes. Lowering her gaze, she saw his cock, still hard.

"Now let me bring you a greater rapture," he

stated.

Her climax had been pleasant, but already she was hungry for more, for greater. She stood up and grasped his member, savoring the hardness in her hand. Her cunnie was indeed partial to this shaft. She caressed the smoothness of the rod and, with her thumb, swept over the drop of seed at the tip. Wordlessly, she gently pulled and pressed her hand down the length, eliciting a grunt of appreciation from him. With a patience she did not expect she had, given that her own cravings had reignited, she fondled him till he, too, climbed the pinnacle of euphoria. But before he could reach the summit, she withdrew. She grabbed his cock and cods in one hand and sharply slapped them with the other. He grunted in surprise and pain.

"Are you my whore, Harry?" she asked in low, husky tones.

He frowned.

"Did you not bid me to use you as one might use a whore?"

She licked at his nipple.

"Aye, Captain."

She propped a foot on the bed behind him

and ground herself onto his right thigh. He bent the leg to give her a better angle to rub her cunnie against. The sensation of flesh against flesh sent currents rippling through her. Her wetness allowed her to glide easily along him. Using his arm as an anchor, she pulled herself up his leg, smearing her moisture upon his thigh. She pressed down harder as the delicious pressure built toward a peak.

"Spend upon me, Captain," he snarled. "Spend upon your whore."

She erupted into divine tremors, holding onto him as her legs weakened. Harry gave a growl, and before she could collect herself from the flood of bliss, he had snapped the left bedpost, scooped her in his freed arm, around the right bedpost and pinned her to the bed beneath his hard and heavy body. She felt his cock, and the rope about him, between her thighs. Desire pumped madly in her veins. She grabbed his head and crushed his lips down to hers. They kissed as if famished for the taste of the other. The intensity was bruising, suffocating. She could not catch a breath, but neither could she stop. She was drowning but would not save herself.

He moved his hips, rubbing himself against her. She groaned, the hollowness between her legs desperately needing to be filled.

"Fuck me," she mumbled against his lips.

"What be you wanting, Captain?" he asked as he took mouthfuls of her neck.

She wanted to punch him—he knew exactly what she had said—but she couldn't deliver a good blow from where she was. Instead, she tangled her fingers in his hair and yanked as hard as she could.

"I said, 'fuck me.'"

His grinned. "As you wish, Captain."

With a single thrust of his hips, he buried nearly his entire length inside her. She gave a harsh gasp at being filled so quickly, so fully. His eyes glimmered.

And though she had yet to adjust to him, not wanting him to think he had bested her, she raised her hips and took in the remaining inches.

He muttered an oath before slowly withdrawing his cock till the tip rested against her outer folds. She took the opportunity to inhale much needed air before he rammed himself back into her. She cried out as her body cramped and the coarse fibers of the rope rubbed her clit. She dug her nails into his back and tried to breathe through the pain. His second thrust was gentle, but she did not lighten her grasp. To her surprise, he pumped with deliberation. She would've thought he would take advantage of his superior position to thrust into her with only his end in mind. But as before, his rhythm and angle of penetration were exactly what her arousal needed. The pain melded with pleasure, and she even came to enjoy the rub of the rope against her. She rolled her hips to his thrusts.

As desire mounted, threatening to overwhelm her, she dug her nails deeper into his flesh. He stilled, compelling her to take over the work. With frenzied desperation, she impaled herself upon his cock over and over. When the summit was in sight for her, he shoved his full-length into her with such force that she thought she would topple from the bed. With her head hanging over the edge, she clawed the scars upon his back as he pummeled into her. The pain was exquisite, the pleasure divine. He covered her mouth with his hand to muffle the screams she could not prevent from escaping her throat as her body hurled toward rapture. She feared what was to come, as if her body were being thrown at a stone wall twenty feet tall and several feet thick, though she knew the wall would burst into pieces upon impact, and the pleasure dammed behind it would be worth the destruction of her body.

Her scream reached a silent pitch when she breached that wall. A blinding euphoria bowled through her, rendering her body useless for anything save shaking and convulsing. Her teeth chattered as Harry propped himself up on both arms and continued to pound away. Eventually she found her voice and practically sobbed at the rapture pressing and pulling her body in every direction.

She remained in the state for several minutes as another tide rose behind the first one. Grinding and shoving himself into her, Harry compelled the second, equally unforgiving, wave to overtake the first, crashing and tumbling her body into violent spasms. She wondered that her body could hold all of it or that she would ever find the surface. Only when Harry pulled out of her did she finally find relief.

With half the broken bedpost dangling from

his wrist, he came up on his knees and fisted his cock. She knew not if it was the earlier denial of spending or the rope cinching his cock and scrotum that delayed his climax. It took several minutes before his seed erupted from his cock. He could have spent inside her, and she, exhausted, would not have stopped him. But she would have had to punish him severely if he had.

After he had milked the last drop from his shaft, he pulled her more fully onto the bed, then reached over and untied himself from the other bedpost. She noticed droplets of red upon the bedclothes beside her. He had bled onto her bed. She felt mildly sorry that she had dug her nails that deeply into him. But he had suffered worse at her hands. An odd sensation, not unlike gratitude, warmed her. She had tested his loyalty, and he had passed. As she watched him unwind the rope about his shaft and cods, she wondered what other manner of devilry she could impose upon him.

He found her gaze, and her breath hitched at the smolder in his eyes. The wolf was still hungry. Her pulse quickened, but she smirked to hide her trepidation. But he knew that what existed between them had changed. They both knew that this was not to be their last tumble.

In Harry, she had found her match, her equal in lust and wickedness.

THE END

A MORE WICKED SEA
(coming spring 2019)

In this dark and erotic sequel to A Wicked Sea, pirate Captain Marinette La Croix sails further into the dark passions between her and Harry Edge, her first mate and the only man whom she has ever given her body to. Together, they push their carnal desires to scorching, wicked heights.

But betrayal looms on the horizon.

La Croix faces a mutiny aboard the Bloody Baron. And the man leading the charge is none other than Harry, the one man she trusted above all others. He's after more than her ship, and she may end up paying the price with her body...

She should have known better than to trust a pirate.

CLAIMING A PIRATE

Excerpt

CHAPTER ONE

~ The Golden Age ~

OF ALL THE WAYS TO DIE, Adanya never thought it would be by sea. A blade through the heart by a traitorous crewman, perhaps. Swaying at the end of a hangman's noose, very likely. Old age, certainly. But not by sea. Not by the mistress she had feared and revered for nigh on three and ten years, since first she had been put to sea at the tender age of nine.

As she lay floating in her bateau with her breeches and shirt shredded, her salt-sprayed hair tangled and plastered about her bruised face, Adanya marveled at how serene the sea felt. Last night, the sea had heaved and pitched in fury as if in battle with the storm clouds above. Now a blue, cloudless sky stretched the length of the horizon, and the sea rolled and sighed like a satisfied lover who had just mended a quarrel.

She shielded her eyes from the glaring midday sun, but the movement made her ribs ache where grapeshot had skimmed her flesh. A dull throb persisted from the blow her quartermaster had dealt to her head, but she preferred these pains to the wrenching of her heart when she considered the fate of her ship, the *Sea Falcon*, and her crew.

"They'll hang us all—if we live," Adanya had shouted to her quartermaster, Damon, as a chain shot flew above them, tearing into the rigging. The *HMS Forte,* a fourth rate, had been battering the *Falcon* for over an hour, finding her aim despite the darkness of night.

Adanya meant her words, but an ugly doubt wormed through her. Not of Death. An early visit from that angel was inevitable for most pirates. And for her and the crew of the *Sea Falcon*, they had all but made a pact with Death. She could almost relish dangling from Gallows Point, but more dreadful to her than the tar, feather and gibbets was the prospect that the British would not even dignify her with the fate of Charles Vane or Jack Rackham, perhaps choosing to burn her at the stake as if she were a common witch instead of the dread pirate who had amassed the largest collective bounty on her head.

"Or worse," she added beneath her breath, the words lost in the wind raging about them.

But Damon seemed to hear it nonetheless and, despite the darkness, she saw clearly in his eyes that he would sooner lie at the bottom of the sea than be sold back into slavery—a sentiment shared, no doubt, by the rest of her crew.

"What now, Cap'n?" Damon demanded.

Like her, he would betray no fear. She scanned her crew — all dedicated, all family to her. They, and the purpose that propelled her reason to live, had done much to relieve the hollow left by one Dominic Bold.

The wind, behaving like a wild banshee, howled at her, throwing droplets of rain into her face that stung like pellets of stone. But the storm was the least of their concerns. They had as many men at the pumps as could be had and still the *Falcon* was taking in water. The *Forte* was pulling up on the starboard side. Within half an hour, His Majesty's Navy would be boarding the *Falcon*. Their small but mighty crew would be no match for the number of men aboard the *Forte*.

"We fight," she declared to Damon, drawing her cutlass and biting back the burst of pain at her side.

157

Damon grunted. "Ye can escape, Cap'n. We can hold 'em off. Ye can sail off in a bateau. They'll not see you in the dark."

Adanya shot Damon an admonishing glare. "I would sooner writhe in Davey Jones' locker than live a coward to watch my brothers die."

"We reckoned that to be our fate when we joined ye" Damon shouted. "If ye lived, ye can assemble a new crew. Find a new ship. Carry on the dream of yer father."

For a moment, Adanya hesitated. Was she being selfish for wanting to die in the comforting company of her crew? Vain for not wanting to be a coward? Weak because the prospect of starting anew daunted her? Was she already a coward for knowing that she could not bear the grief she would suffer, were she to survive and all else perished, leaving her an empty shell whose bowels had been ripped from her? She had no wish to die alone and in such a state.

"I go down with the ship, Damon," she said. "Have the men find whatever weaponry they can."

She turned to shed her coat. The garment, weighted by rain, would hinder her in close combat.

"Sorry, Cap'n."

Damon had mumbled the words, and before she could ascertain what he meant, she was thrown into a deeper darkness.

* * * * *

The sun peered over the horizon, its glow bringing the promise of another warm day. She had spent the previous day drifting in a daze. Adanya eyed the apparition of a ship in the distance. Already she was suffering delusions. What were the chances the *Sea Falcon* had escaped the *HMS Forte*? The *Falcon* was one of the fastest ships but had sustained heavy damage.

The hull of the ship advancing towards her was too wide to be the *Falcon*, the tonnage not enough to be the *Forte*. Perhaps it wasn't a mirage. Adanya sat up.

A schooner. Even without full sails unfurled in all her glory, the approaching vessel had grandeur to her. Adanya admired the ship, from the tip of the bowsprit to the top of its mainmast. No flags flew from its mast tops. No pendants. Then it wasn't a war ship. Perhaps a privateer.

Or...another pirate.

Making out the figurehead, Adanya fell back onto the planks with a groan, willing the sea to swallow her whole at that moment.

Of all the miserable luck. Of all the people, it had to be *him*.

She heard rather than saw the ship pulling abreast. And though nearly five years had passed, a voice more familiar than her own reached her ears.

"Well, well...Captain Mbwana."

She could hear the grin in the way he spoke. She kept her eyes closed, as if hoping to wake to a different fate.

"Would you be needin' a hand?"

Her eyes snapped open to find a pair of dark eyes laced with mirth gazing down at her. Damn. Dominic Bold was as handsome as she last remembered—mayhap more.

The sun's rays played on his auburn hair with russet glints. Dressed in a blue coat with trim, the top buttons of his shirt undone to reveal the muscular ridges of his chest, and with but two days' growth of beard on his rugged chin, he looked particularly refreshed and debonair. Dominic had always looked half gentleman, half pirate. She was struck by how miserable she must have looked in comparison.

"Only a fool need ask," she called back as she rose to her feet and reached into the water for the rope that had been thrown down the side of the ship for her.

"'Tis an honor to have the illustrious Captain Mbwana aboard the *Phantom*," Dominic said once two of his crew had hauled her onto the deck. He bowed with a grandeur befitting a king's court.

Adanya moved her gaze from the muscular leg he presented up the length of his broad chest and shoulders. When she met his eyes, the half-smile on his face indicated he had seen her appreciative sweep of his body.

She quickly changed her focus to the ship. Except for the addition of another square topsail, a new topgallant on her foremast, and new faces among the crew, the *Phantom* looked much as it did the last time she had been aboard. She found comfort in the familiarity, and as much as he unsettled her, there was comfort in Dominic as well.

She was handed a flask of water, which she tried not to swig too swiftly in her thirst.

"I shall have our quartermaster arrange a cabin for you," Dominic informed her. "It won't be what you're accustomed to—"

"Anything will do, thank ye," Adanya said. She almost reminded him of where she used to sleep— with the crew of the *Phantom*—but decided not to bring up the past. She did not trust herself to venture there, and she could not decide if she was relieved or hurt that he could muster such a blithe tone, as if they were about to sit down to bloody tea, as if they did not share a past.

"I take it you won't be needin' your, er, vessel?" he inquired.

Adanya looked down at the bateau that had served as her home for the last two days. An ache filled her heart. What if that was all that remained of the *Sea Falcon*?

As if reading her mind, Dominic dropped his humor and said, "We passed her a day ago, a British warship in pursuit but losing ground by the hour. That were a fine fast ship you have."

Relief flooded her—and then a swelling of pride. He approved of her ship. The smile on his lips indicated he was glad to be the bearer of good news.

She felt a sudden urge to bring those lips down upon her own.

An uneasy warmth surged in her loins as she recalled how it once felt to have his mouth consume hers. Their gazes connected, and suddenly it seemed as if they were the only two people in the world and five years had melted into none.

"Captain Bold?"

Adanya looked past Dominic to find the source of the sweet, feminine voice was a beautiful redheaded woman, wearing a yellow and ivory gown that displayed slender sloping shoulders and a small waist. With alabaster skin, rouged cheeks, and soft and supple flesh, the woman was the mirror opposite of Adanya, whose years of working on a ship had further darkened her ebony skin and hardened her flesh into toned muscle.

"I see you've not given up your taste for wenches," Adanya noted, trying to keep the jealousy out of her voice. She licked her own chapped lips to make them less unsightly before the rosy lips of the other woman.

"Old habits die hard—or not at all," Dominic replied. He turned to the gentlewoman. "Miss Wrenwood, I present to you Captain Adanya Mbwana."

Miss Wrenwood bobbed a curtsy. "Pleased to meet you, sir."

Adanya stiffened, though she could not fault the woman for thinking her a man. Not only was she dressed in a shirt and breeches, but her bosom, as was her custom, was bound to disguise her form. Her crew knew her to be a woman, but they did not need reminders of her womanhood.

"Captain Mbwana has the current honor of being the scourge of the Atlantic," Dominic praised. "The English have placed a bounty on her head of no less than twenty thousand quid."

"Her?" Miss Wrenwood echoed, her eyes searching Adanya with obvious doubt.

"Surely the bounty on *your* head differs little," Adanya returned graciously.

"Alas, I am told that I am worth but five thousand nowadays."

"Then," said Miss Wrenwood to Dominic, "he— she, is a pirate as well?"

This time Adanya bowed but kept her gaze on Dominic. "I learned from the best, m'lady."

"Too well," Dominic replied with foreboding. He turned to a bearded man he addressed as Mr. Collins and told him to set an extra place at the captain's table for supper.

"My first mate will see you to your quarters," Dominic said to Adanya.

"Rowland Stirling, at your service," greeted a tall man with soft hair and icy blue eyes.

The first mate was almost as attractive as Dominic, but in Adanya's eyes, Dominic was a near perfect specimen of man, being a perfect blend of his mother and father. Dominic's dark eyes and full lashes came from his French mother, a beautiful woman whose portraiture Adanya had seen in Dominic's cabin. The broad shoulders, expansive chest, and skin that bronzed easily in the sun Dominic inherited from his father, a Mongol pirate.

Dominic bowed, then offered his arm to Miss Wrenwood and led her away. Adanya watched their departing backs. She wanted to retch.

"I shall have a set of clothes brought to you," Rowland said as he showed Adanya below deck and opened the door to a small but well-lighted cabin. "I am sure Miss Wrenwood would spare a gown—"

"I've not worn a gown but once in me life," Adanya interrupted, "and no desire to do so again."

It wasn't entirely true. She could well remember the way Dominic had looked at her that day she had dug up a gown from a recent pillage. He had looked at her differently, no longer as his pilot, but as a *woman*. Adanya would have given anything to see his eyes light up in the same manner once more.

But gown or not, she knew she could not hold sway over his attentions as well as the likes of Miss Wrenwood. She imagined Dominic running his hands through Miss Wrenwood's long silken tresses. He could not do the same with her motley hair.

And to her horror, she felt the tentacles of jealousy gripping her once more. How she loathed that feeling. Five years should have squelched such sentiments.

"Be you wantin' anything...?" Rowland asked with a restrained but eerie eagerness. His eyes bore into her as if he sought to unearth her secrets.

"Nay," Adanya replied, meeting his stare. Rowland would be a devilishly handsome man but for the subtle sneer upon his lips. He wore his light brown hair streaked with flaxen in a loose queue, a single earring of gold through an ear, and two pistols at his sides. She wondered why the man armed himself when walking about his own ship and imagined he was the kind to sleep with one eye open. A man who trusted no one could not himself be trusted.

She went to stand by the door, waiting for him to leave. He smiled—to her or himself, she knew not, but cared little that he should find amusement in her.

"If there be anything," he said as he stepped outside, "we are at your service."

He began an awkward bow, but he lacked the grace that Dominic, a man of many worlds, could conjure. She shut the door in the middle of his bow.

Alone, she sat down on her bed and released the groans and grimaces that she, not wanting to reveal the slightest weakness before Dominic, had forced inside. She put her head in her hands. She had to find a way back to her ship.

But most of all, she had to get away from Dominic and all the terrible wrenching feelings that knotted her guts whenever her gaze met his. His tone had been lighthearted enough, but she knew he had not buried the past any more than she had.

OTHER WORKS BY EM BROWN

His For A Week Series
Bought
Ravaged
Tormented
Devastated

Erotic Contemporary Short Stories
Damien
And Damien Makes Four

Cavern of Pleasure Series
Mastering the Marchioness
Conquering the Countess
Binding the Baroness
Lord Barclay's Seduction

Red Chrysanthemum Stories
Master vs. Mistress
Master vs. Mistress: The Challenge Continues
Seducing the Master
Taking the Temptress
Master vs. Temptress: The Final Submission
A Wedding Night Submission
Punishing Miss Primrose, Parts I – XX
The Submission of Lady Pennington

Made in the USA
Middletown, DE
16 March 2024

51641330R00095